The Secret of Lakeham Abbey

Sally Quilford

CROOKED
CAT

First Black Line Edition, Crooked Cat Publishing Ltd. 2016

Discover us online:
www.crookedcatpublishing.com

Join us on facebook:
www.facebook.com/crookedcatpublishing

*Tweet a photo of yourself holding
this book to @crookedcatbooks
and something nice will happen.*

To my wonderful dad, Idris Peploe,
who taught me to love reading.

Acknowledgements

There are so many people I want to thank, and so little space in which to do it. I've already dedicated this book to my wonderful dad. It is fair to say that without him I would not be a writer. He taught me to love reading, starting me off on Jack Higgins, Alistair MacLean, Frederick Forsyth and Nevil Shute. Mixing these influences with the Barbara Cartland and Mills & Boon romances I read at my aunties' houses, is probably what led to me writing so much romantic intrigue.

I would also like to thank the VWs, and the WWs, my two separate sets of 'sisters' who guide me through life's troubles. You all know who you are!

Thank you also to my wonderful friends on Facebook, who cheer and support my efforts and have done so for a long time now.

Thank you to the fab Sue Barnard, who nagged me for ages to send a novel to Crooked Cat. Only my own fear of failure stopped me from doing so for so long, but her belief in me has been unstinting. Thank you, Stephanie and Laurence Patterson, for taking a chance on me. Special thanks to my lovely and sympathetic editor, Maureen Vincent-Northam, for her invaluable input in bringing this novel up to scratch.

Finally thank you to my wonderful husband, children and grandchildren, just for being there to remind me I'm not alone when I come out of a story-induced haze.

The Author

Sally Quilford left school in 1979 with no qualifications, after a peripatetic childhood which resulted in her going to many different schools, or a lot of the time not going to school at all. Despite that, she still managed to be able to read and write very well, and always loved English. At the age of 30, whilst sitting the bath (where all her best ideas happen), Sally had an epiphany and returned to education, eventually earning 5 GCSEs and a 2.1 Hons. degree in Humanities and Literature from the Open University. At the same time, she finally started to write, after years of thinking she 'might try it', starting with poetry and fan-fiction.

Her first efforts are lost to time and the vagaries of computer formatting. In 2007, Sally decided it was time to start taking things more seriously and was determined to earn money from her writing. That year, she earned £10 for a letter in a woman's magazine. However, it focussed her mind on improving her craft. Since then, she has had well over 60 short stories published in magazines in Britain and abroad, countless articles, and over 20 pocket novels, published by either DC Thomson or Linford Romance Library.

Sally is a member of the Romantic Novelists' Association and serves on its committee, organising their bi-annual parties and the Awards reception. She has previously worked as an advisor at a Law Centre and the Citizens Advice Bureau.

Though born in South Wales, Sally now lives in Derbyshire with her husband and two West Highland Terriers.

Follow Sally at http://sallyquilford.blogspot.co.uk!

The Secret of
Lakeham Abbey

Chapter One

Percy Sullivan
Aged 14

This is the story of that summer at Lakeham Abbey. I intend, through thorough (detailed, systematic) investigation of the facts, to clear a woman of a heinous crime. I like that word; heinous. It means monstrous, atrocious, odious, and terrible and so on. I got that from the Roget's Thesaurus that Mother bought me for Christmas. They say there isn't a synonym for thesaurus, which is supposed to be ironic, but they're wrong. It's onomasticon, which means a dictionary of synonyms and antonyms.

The boys at school laugh at me when I say this sort of thing out loud – it isn't the done thing to show that one is too clever – so I've learned to keep quiet in class. But this is my journal, so I think I can say whatever I want without worrying about anyone teasing me.

They're good chaps and all that and they know they can't go too far with the razzing (teasing, joshing) because of my wheelchair. The problem is that they can do so many things I can't, like play soccer and rugby, and go on cross country runs. They hate it, and complain all the time, but they don't realise what it's like not to be able to do those things and how lucky they are that they can. When they're playing sports or running they're a team and they all share the same experience, even if it means getting bruised and muddy. Not one of them can share my experience, so they don't really understand me. Father says I'm lucky that my brain still works otherwise I'd have been put in a very different institution.

Going back to the heinous crime, I have contacted

everyone who was involved in the events at Lakeham Abbey and asked them to write down their version of what happened.

That includes Mother and Father, Group Captain Marsh, Doctor Aitken and the Carstairs. And Anne Pargeter, of course. (My teacher says I shouldn't start a sentence with and, but as I've already said, this is my journal so I will write as I please.) There are others, who came and went, but I can't find them all and I'm not sure their English is very good anyway.

It all happened just after the war. I hadn't been to the country since I was a refugee, and that only lasted a couple of weeks, until the family sent me back home. It's not my fault that I realised the farmer's wife was having an affair with one of the shepherds. Perhaps it would have been better if I hadn't told him… So I spent most of the war in London, listening to the bombs dropping every night. It was fun really, though Mother was not too keen.

When the war ended and we could start moving around safely again, Father said it would be nice to get away for a few months because London is mostly a pile of rubble. The other kids like that as they can go exploring. One chap in our block of flats found an unexploded bomb! I can't do anything like that. But I can use my brain, so that's what I'm going to do to help Anne.

Apart from one horrible event at Lakeham Abbey, we had a lovely time. Most of the reason for that is because Anne was there and she knew how to make people happy. She always said and did the right thing, and was brilliant at giving us lots of cake and other yummy food. Mostly black market, but none of us really minded that. Then things became dire (calamitous, disastrous) and Anne was taken away. It was the worst day of my life and I've been woeful ever since. (I think woeful is a much better word than miserable, because people can be miserable just because they got out of bed the wrong side, but woeful suggests something really awful must have happened.)

Somewhere amongst all the people who visited the Abbey that summer is a killer (murderer, assassin) and I will find out who it is. There isn't much time. Anne will soon be hanged (dangled, suspended) for murder and I must put a stop to it.

Also, if I can stop the execution, I reckon Jennifer Carstairs will think I'm a hero and like me better.

Celia Sullivan
(Percy's mother)

I'm not sure I should even be doing this. Percy has already been distressed by the events. He loves Anne so dearly, and refuses to believe the worst of her. I don't want him to be hurt anymore. But I promised to help him, and after what happened in the past, I owe him the truth.

It feels odd, talking about things he already knows, but there are things he doesn't know. How will he react if he finds out the truth about why he's in the wheelchair? He may never forgive me…

The annoying thing now is that everyone says that they could have warned me about Anne Pargeter. But it wasn't like that before we went to Lakeham Abbey for the summer. Oh no. Then it was all, "Oh, you must try Anne Pargeter, darling Celia. She's an absolute marvel." When the aunt of one of Bunty's friends broke her leg skiing – such a silly pastime for a woman in her seventies – Anne Pargeter had her back on her feet in a fortnight. Or it might have been a couple of months. But all agreed then that Anne Pargeter was the cat's pyjamas. She was a bit of a Jill-of-all-trades. Nannying, governessing, housekeeping.

"She makes sure everyone's ship sails smoothly," Bunty informed me.

"What? Is she some sort of Wren? We don't have a ship, Bunty. We'll be staying in a house." I've never been very good at metaphors.

"You need help, Celia," Bunty said. "You're pretty useless as a mother."

I was going through a phase where I wanted to bring Percy and Lily up by myself, without the help of a nanny. After all, nannies can be so troublesome, with their love lives and their wanting at least one day off a week. So I thought I might as well do it all by myself. I suppose I wanted to prove that I could do it. We still had Henry, Percy's attendant, but I was not fond of girls who looked at me in a superior manner, because they were better at childcare than I was.

Unfortunately, that was closely followed by what my husband, Freddie, now calls 'The Incident'. It was not entirely my fault, I'm sure. I was in Harrods and the girl was trying to persuade me to buy either Ivory Satin or Porcelain Beige, and I'm convinced that they're both exactly the same shade, so could not make up my mind. Percy would have known, because he's very clever, but he was in boarding school at the time.

The next thing you know, Bunty comes back from the linen department, saying she is in a hurry because she has to get back to her gallery, and we're in the taxi and I am still trying to decide which was the best foundation, and I had the awful feeling I'd forgotten something. I couldn't for the life of me remember what. I was halfway home when I realised that I'd left Lily in her pram in the cosmetics department.

The police were awfully nice. "These things happen all the time, madam," I was assured.

"They do where Celia is concerned," said Bunty, which I thought was rather uncalled for. What happened with Percy's legs was not my fault. Besides, I'd managed not to lose him at all. And even if I had, he is rather clever and could easily find his way home. I fear Lily will not be as bright. I said as much to Bunty.

"Perhaps you could have waited till she was a bit older to test that notion," she suggested, which made

Freddie tsk in that irritated way he has whenever Bunty visits.

I sometimes think Freddie looks down on me. In fact, I sometimes wonder why he married me at all. He's terribly clever, with his grasp of all things Egyptian. Or Greek. That's why we took Lakeham Abbey. So he could write his treatise on Tuscan pottery. No, not Tuscan. The other one. Etruscan. I always think history would be much easier if they didn't use such similar sounding words. Like the Hittites and Hitler. How is one supposed to know they're not the same thing?

Freddie had taken the house for the summer. He promised there would be plenty of room for the children to play, and we would have houseguests. It would be a proper house party such as my parents used to have before the war killed all our servants and Mother and Father had to sell up and move abroad because of the awful government expecting them to pay taxes.

I had always wanted to host such a party, but I feared I could not do that and be an attentive mother at the same time.

Anyway, that was when my friend Bunty mentioned Anne Pargeter. This is sadly ironic when you consider the way things turned out. "Celia, darling, if you can't manage two children in a three-bedroom flat in London, how on earth are you going to keep tabs on them in a fifty-room gothic pile in the country? She'll sort out the children and the guests. All you have to do is sit back and relax. She's not cheap, mind you…"

That was alright, because Freddie, despite only being a professor of archaeology at Oxford, is well looked after by our cousin, the Duke of Marsholm. The Duke funds most of Freddie's digs, and he promised to pay for Lakeham Abbey for the summer so that Freddie could write his book. I reasoned that I could include Miss Pargeter's salary in with the household accounts.

"Send her to me," I ordered, already enjoying being in a position to give such orders. I felt that I should like being the grand dame of a country home.

What did I think of Anne Pargeter? Well, I have to admit I thought she seemed a very pleasant young lady. She was twenty-nine years old, if I remember correctly from her application. Some have asked if I realised that her hair was dyed blonde. I don't think I gave it much thought. And even if it was dyed, having blonde hair is hardly proof of being a murderer. Lily is blonde and I'm sure she will grow up to be a very nice girl, even if she doesn't always know her way home.

"How many will be in the party?" This was the first question Anne asked me at our interview.

"Oh, let me see. There will be me, my husband Freddie, and our two children. Percy is twelve and Lily is two. My friend, Bunty, but she will be coming and going. She has a gallery in Knightsbridge and if she turns her back on it for two minutes the girls have extra tea breaks and sneak their boyfriends in the back. Then there's Doctor Stanley Aitken, who helps me with my nerves. Who else? Oh yes, Group Captain Guy Marsh. He's related to us in some way. I forget how. Guy has been unwell since the war, so he's coming to convalesce. He more or less invited himself. There will be others coming and going. The Carstairs. Angus, Emma and their daughter, Jennifer. They're looking for a property in the area. Angus is the local Member of Parliament so he needs a constituency house. We have promised to put them up whilst they look. How many is that?"

"Ten so far. Seven adults and three children. Plus, other guests popping in every now and then. Will Group Captain Marsh require a special diet?"

"Oh, how do I know? He was shot down, but not in the stomach I don't think. You may eat with us, if we don't have visitors. At least that's what my own governess used to do." I felt a little apologetic, because Anne Pargeter was clearly a cut above the usual governess.

"That is more than satisfactory." She nodded,

graciously.

"I suppose," I hesitated, "that the men will want meat. Only it's so hard with the rationing and…" It's always difficult to bring up the subject of using the black market with servants. Many of them are so funny about being involved with crime and the police. "The Duke will send down some pheasants I'm sure. Or grouse. Maybe something from his farm but…"

"Don't worry, Mrs Sullivan. I have contacts that will ensure plenty of food. I presume the children will take their meals in the nursery."

"Yes, I suppose they will." I must say that Anne could sometimes make one feel a little inadequate as I had given no thought at all to where the children might eat. In the London flat they always ate with us, because we only had the one room in which to dine, unless we had guests in which case they ate early and went to bed. "Percy won't like it, but he's too young to sit in at dinner with guests. You have to watch Lily. She has a habit of getting herself lost. The last time was in Harrods." I didn't elaborate. After all, I barely knew Anne Pargeter.

"Goodness." She laughed, and it was a rather nice, restful sound. "A spirited child, then?"

I liked that. It made me feel less neglectful. "Yes, indeed."

"So," she said, starting to put her gloves back on. "My duties will include sorting out the children, their meals and entertainments, and also making sure all the adults are catered for. I imagine your husband will want quiet time for his research, and that you may want special events, like picnics and garden parties?"

"Yes, indeed." I had thought of neither picnic nor garden party, but both sounded very appealing. I immediately saw myself as the hostess, dressed in gossamer, gliding amongst the guests like one of the swans in *Swan Lake*.

"Will there be other staff on hand to help with cleaning and general duties?"

"Oh yes, they're employed by the owners. I'm not sure if there is a cook."

"I know of a good cook, so don't worry about that, Mrs Sullivan. Will I also be responsible for arranging their duties? With special consideration to your wishes, of course."

"Of course." That was better. She seemed to be forgetting who was boss! Actually, I was forgetting who was boss and I must say it's a very liberating sensation to have someone else take on all the responsibility. And the thinking. Thinking is very hard sometimes, though I know Freddie and Percy do a lot of it. Anne Pargeter seemed to be rather good at it. So much so that she appeared to know what I wanted before I even knew I wanted it.

"That sounds suitable," she said with a smile. "I can go on ahead, if you wish, to ensure that everything is ready for you. Just let me know what you want for dinner on the night of your arrival and we'll make up the rest as we go along, shall we?"

"Oh, could you do all that, Anne? That would be helpful and..." I suddenly realised that I had not even offered her the job. In fact, I was not sure I had done the interviewing. The next thing I knew, I was giving her an advance on her wages so that she could take the train to Lakeham Abbey, and all I had to do was turn up and make it look as though I had thought of it all.

How could one complain about such a capable young woman? Someone, I forget who, said that Anne Pargeter's links to the black market and her organisational abilities make her a prime suspect for murder. But how was I to know that on the very first day I met her? It was not on her résumé.

I know that Percy does not want to believe this, but sometimes people are not what they seem. I do fear that this little project of his will needlessly distress him.

Professor Frederick Sullivan

(Percy's father)

Anne Pargeter? It's a sorry affair all around and I really think it would be better to leave well alone. She seemed a decent enough girl. Not showy or trashy in any way. Good legs, if I remember rightly. Not that I'd want Celia to know I noticed. She does worry somewhat that I'll one day run off with a clever woman. But who wants a clever woman? It can make a man feel…well…not a man…if you know what I mean.

I didn't meet Miss Pargeter until we went to Lakeham Abbey. I left the hiring to Celia. That was a bit of a risk, I know, but she didn't do too badly. To begin with, Anne was eminently suitable for the post. Celia couldn't have known the girl was a bad 'un, could she?

I didn't notice her hair was dyed. Who does notice these things? Other women might, but I've no idea. When one spends all one's life digging holes and indexing pottery, one has little understanding of peroxide and the other wiles women use to ensnare us chaps. Not that I think Miss Pargeter was trying to ensnare anyone. She got a bit close to Guy Marsh at one point, but he wants nothing to do with her now. As for him and Celia…well…I'm still not sure what's happening there. They seem to have their heads together a lot nowadays. That's a bit worrying…

I'd taken Lakeham Abbey so that I could finish my book. I was also going to liaise with some men bringing pottery from abroad. I was to catalogue it and then see that it got into the museums. It was not a great use of my skills, but who could go on archaeological digs with Europe still in turmoil? So I had to take whatever work I could get.

Back to Anne Pargeter. She fooled us all in the end. She had murder in her heart and I thank God that they caught her before the children were harmed. Percy had already been through so much, what with his legs. What damned bad luck brought someone so evil into our household?

11

Chapter Two

Doctor Stanley Aitken
(Mrs Sullivan's physician)

I hear young Percy Sullivan is trying to do a bit of sleuthing. Well, why not? It's good for a boy to have a hobby. He wants to be careful he doesn't dig too deep, though. These things have a way of turning bad.

I wasn't at Lakeham Abbey enough to make any firm decisions as to the guilt or innocence of Anne Pargeter. I only stayed for a few nights each week, or more often than not, the weekend, but my practice took me elsewhere. I don't think the Sullivans always understood that. Those who can live off trust funds and the charity of rich relations seldom understand the struggles of those of us who have to work for a living. I could hardly be expected to care for Mrs Sullivan for nothing, even if she was offering me board and lodge for the summer.

That being said, Celia and Freddie Sullivan are a charming couple. She is a simple, sweet creature; a thoroughly fine woman. Even though she seemed slightly scatty at times, I had no doubt that if backed into a corner she would kill for her husband and children.

I must admit that I did not recognise Anne Pargeter at first. Not only was she twenty-nine years old, but she had changed her hair. As a child, her hair, if I remember rightly, had been what they call strawberry blonde, but is really ginger. When I met her again as an adult, she had dyed it blonde. That rather white blonde that actresses favour, which is not surprising under the circumstances. She also wore thick foundation, which covered the freckles across her pretty nose. She still managed to be a pretty and fresh looking girl, but that only shows how much she deceived us all. I don't think she recognised me, at least at first.

It is a tragic tale all around and I am sure everyone will have seen newspaper reports detailing the whole, sordid story. I hope it has not been too upsetting for young Percy. He was very fond of the girl. Nevertheless, I think he should give up his attempts to save her. It will only bring him anguish and none of us want to see that.

I am going to speak under the basis of it is better to be cruel to be kind. It is my belief that the Good Lord always punishes the guilty and that, for her sins, Anne Pargeter is exactly where she deserves to be. May God have mercy on her soul.

Group Captain Guy Marsh
(Relation of the Sullivans)

I'd like to help my young friend, Hotspur, really, I would. But there's very little I can tell that he doesn't already know. I understand he has this whole Wilkie Collins thing going on, asking for our testimonies, but I am not sure I can add anything to the story. It's a tricky one. I like the lad a lot, and I don't want to tell him to get lost.

Truth is that I was taken in by Anne Pargeter just as everyone else was. It's rather a sore subject with me. When I came back from the war injured, I was afflicted with what they call survivor's guilt, wondering why I had lived when so many others had died, and for a short while she helped me see past that and hope for a brighter future. But it was all an illusion. She was not who she pretended to be.

I have no idea why she used me the way she did. Perhaps she thought it amusing to ensnare me.

Damn, this is so hard. I don't want to ruin Hotspur's memories of her. I do believe that she did care for him and little Lily and that she would not have harmed them. Perhaps that's something he can hold on to in these dark

13

days. I promised to take him flying, so I could help take his mind off things with that.

It would be better for everyone involved if he just left the Anne Pargeter business alone. I know I wish that I had.

Anne Pargeter
(Writing From Holloway Prison)

Dearest Hotspur, I was so pleased to receive your letter and it warms my heart that you want to fight so hard for my freedom. I think your idea to get everyone to write down their own thoughts on the events of our time at Lakeham Abbey is awfully clever.

As clever as it is, I must urge you to give up this quest of yours. Time is running out, my dearest, and I do not want you to spend that time agonising over my fate. You have your whole life ahead of you, and you won't be in that wheelchair forever, despite what the doctors say. You are capable of doing so many great things. If you align yourself with me, that scandal will harm you for the rest of your life, and I have no wish to do that.

People will tell you a lot about me, some of it true and some of it false. But know this. I would never have harmed you or Lily. I love you both so dearly.

Forget the darkness, forget me.

If you do choose to remember me, remember all those good times we had at Lakeham Abbey: the walks in the plantation, the picnics on the island with Group Captain Marsh… These are the memories that sustain me in these dark days.

I wonder… Have you seen him? Is he well, do you know?

Please take care of your little sister for me. Your mother tries really hard, despite what people think, but she suffered abuse and manipulation at the hands of a devil for so long that it cannot help but leave its mark.

God bless you, my angel. I think that one day, if heaven allows after you have had a long and fruitful life, we will meet again.

    Love
    Anne
    xxx

Percy Sullivan

No, no, no! They've all done it wrong. All except Anne, and I am sure it is hard for her to write much on prison paper and with the warders reading every word. Even she forgot about the ghost. I am still sure it means something, yet no one thought to mention it. Perhaps Anne does not mention it in case they think she is mad. Which would be better as they can't hang someone who is mad, can they?

How am I ever to clear Anne's name if no one else is able to tell the story properly? Mother waffles on about household preparations and leaving Lily outside Harrods – as if that were a rare occurrence. Father is more interested in his secret sideline, which has nothing to do with this story at all. He thinks I do not know about it, but I'm much cleverer than he thinks.

Doctor Aitken is especially bad at telling a story, revealing in his first missive that he knew Anne when she was a child. That revelation should have come much later in the narrative.

As for Group Captain Marsh, he has let me down more than any of them. I know that Mother is a silly goose and that Father only thinks of his books and pottery, so I expect it from them. The doctor is hardly known to us so I suppose he feels he owes me nothing. But Group Captain Marsh is supposed to be the hero. Yet he dismisses Anne's plight as if it were nothing to him.

If I were him, and not stuck in this stupid wheelchair, I would be flying into the prison grounds and helping her to escape.

If he ever loved her how can he possibly believe that she is a murderer?

Chapter Three

Celia Sullivan

Well, that's a turn up for the books. I asked Freddie about the difference between Etruscan and Tuscan pottery and he said there is none. They come from the same area of Italy. Lord knows why they give it different names. Does this mean that Hitler is one of the Hittites? I meant to ask Freddie, but I forgot.

Anyway, back to the investigation. I shall try to tell things in the right order. I'm a little confused when Percy says that does not necessarily mean chronologically. He tells me that I must give some thought to dramatic effect. I can't say I'm entirely sure what he means but I'll do my best.

I am hardly Virginia Woolf. Which is probably just as well, otherwise I would not understand a word of what I was writing.

I shall also try very hard not to go off on what Percy calls 'flights of fancy' about make-up and shopping in Harrods. Which is unlikely, anyway, because apart from one trip up to London to see his specialist on Harley Street, I had little chance to go shopping for the whole of that summer. We did have that smashing tea at the Ritz that day and then stayed over in a hotel, even though we could have gone back to the flat, I suppose.

Oh dear. Percy will be telling me off for getting ahead of the story again.

Let me start with the first day at Lakeham Abbey. I really do think chronologically is the best way forward. If I try to remember everything from that day I can't get ahead of myself, can I?

I suppose I should give some description of the Abbey. I'm not very good at recognising these things, but I do remember Freddie admiring its gothic features: vaulted ceilings, flying buttresses and gargoyles, and the like. I thought it looked rather dark and forbidding, even though the current owners had done their best to brighten it up inside by knocking some rooms into one to make large airy spaces. Unfortunately, this did make the drawing room rather chilly when the sun went in. I think the house had been a hospital during the war. Sometimes when you walked along a corridor, you could still smell disinfectant and that strange old lady smell one finds in nursing homes.

Anne was very clever about finding coal, just as she easily found things we could not get on ration. It's obvious that she had a criminal bent all along. It did not concern us to begin with because everyone uses the black market for something.

There was also a plantation, though much of the land had been given over to the war effort and was still under government control. At the end of the plantation... (I do hope I'm creating a proper picture, even though Percy has seen it all and doesn't really need to be told.) At the end of the plantation was a lake, rather marshy and a bit slippery in wet weather. Doctor Aitken told us that awful story about the girl who was sucked under and then haunted the house forever after. Or was it someone else who haunted the house? It's all a bit confusing to me.

In the centre of the lake was an island. Percy and Jennifer Carstairs spent a lot of time over there with Anne and Group Captain Marsh, though I do wonder now if I should have put a stop to that. I hate to say it but she was only a servant, and her fraternising with my son, and using him as a chaperone, was not very respectable of her.

Where was I? We had the use of the ground, first and second floor rooms. The third floor and everything above that was out of bounds and there were locked doors at the bottom of the staircases at each end of the house preventing us from going up there. Not that I minded. We had enough room for our guests. Percy was not at all happy to have part of the house shut off to him and he wanted his man, Henry, to break down the door, which Henry, quite rightly, refused to do.

As she had promised, Anne Pargeter went on ahead and had everything waiting for us. I have no idea what contacts she used, and I probably don't want to know, but there was boiled ham for lunch, with a garden salad, and fruit pudding. At dinner we had a leg of lamb, with fresh vegetables and Spotted Dick and real custard for dessert. We did eat very well that summer. Better than we had in all the time we had been on rations.

Anne was waiting at the door for us, with the cook she'd employed; an elderly woman called Maudie. We were introduced first, Freddie and I. Henry was still getting Percy out of the car. He was rather grumpy from the trip, if I remember rightly, because when we introduced him to Anne, who was already holding Lily as if she had known her for years, Percy said, "I don't need a bloody, buggering nanny and I won't eat with the baby."

"Would you rather eat in your room alone?" Anne asked, arching an eyebrow. She had very fine eyebrows – perfectly natural as far as I could see though she did wear her foundation rather heavy. I wondered if it was Ivory Satin or Porcelain Beige and whether she knew the difference.

"No, I would not," Percy said. "I am old enough to sit with the adults."

"I would tend to agree," said Anne. "But sadly that is not possible for either of us, so I do hope you will keep me and Lily company in the nursery, otherwise we would have no intelligent conversation at all."

I wondered why she lied to him, as I had already told her she could sit with us at dinner. I think it was a mark of things to come, and the grand liar she would turn out to be, but it seemed to mollify Percy, and Henry found it amusing, which is strange as he hardly ever smiles, or speaks, for that matter.

I always imagine that when Percy and Henry are alone, they chatter away together quite happily. I wonder if that's the case. Where was I? Oh yes. "Girls talk about stupid things anyway," Percy said.

"Oh, I am sure you are right, Percy," Anne replied. "So it would be wonderful if you could guide us to more intellectual topics."

"I agree." He nodded. "I shall be happy to teach you everything I know." It makes me smile to remember how easily she handled him. Men do like to be flattered about their intelligence.

We were introduced to Maudie, who insisted on calling Miss Pargeter 'Annie', which I felt was rather too familiar. I had a suspicion that Maudie was a secret drinker. She had one of those noses. Like WC Fields. But she made up for it by being an excellent cook.

There was tea and cake waiting for us, to keep us going until lunchtime. It was a very good Victoria Sponge. Percy asked for seconds, which made me so happy as I fear he doesn't eat enough.

Anne had readied all the bedrooms for us. Mine was very pretty, with bright yellow wallpaper. It also overlooked the lake. I had my own sitting room, which was rather luxurious after all the restraints of wartime. Freddie's room was next door, though it's fair to say he spent little time in it. We were used to sharing, you see.

I'm not quite sure where Anne slept during that time. The servants' quarters were blocked off, so they had to sleep in the downstairs bedrooms. This was not quite appropriate, but with all the upstairs doors locked, there was little to be done. I think they were in the East wing, whereas we were in the West wing, so at least we didn't have to run into the parlour maid putting on her pinny first thing in the morning.

I do remember hearing Anne scream that first night, but only because all the windows were open.

Professor Frederick Sullivan

I've already advised Percy not to pursue this matter. It will only bring trouble. Besides, Celia knows more about the domestic help – that being a woman's domain. I am a busy man and quite frankly there are things that happened during our time at Lakeham Abbey that could create problems for all of us.

Celia has just put her head through the door and said, "We must help Percy, even if it does hurt him." She thinks that if we set everything down, he will see the truth of the matter, and then he will no longer doubt that Anne Pargeter is in the right place. Celia has gone off to lunch now with Group Captain Marsh. She says she has something to talk to him about.

Normally I wouldn't mind her having lunch with another man, but he's so dashed handsome and not a dull old stick like me. I sometimes wonder if she's in love with him. It's difficult for a man like me who couldn't prove his worth in the war, what with my club foot. Group Captain Marsh was alright, flying around in his plane, impressing all the ladies. I think Celia is rather more impressed with him than a woman who is married with two children needs to be.

Enough of that. I'm to talk about our first day at Lakeham Abbey, so that's what I'll do. I think Percy fell asleep on the way and was none too happy to be woken when we arrived. Then Anne Pargeter worked her magic with a slice or two of Victoria Sponge and he seemed to chirp up a bit. She was a very efficient girl. A bit too pleased with herself, if you ask me. Women like that frighten me. Not that I was in any way attracted to her, despite her good legs. She looked like one of those early pilgrims, in a black dress with starched white collar. She also wore a bit too much make-up. My wife is naturally beautiful and I'm sure never wears anything more than a dash of lipstick.

It was a rather magnificent house. Built sometime in the fourteenth century, I believe, then knocked down by Henry VIII, then rebuilt and turned into a family home. Sad to say that the Lakehams were not the luckiest of families. Sometime in the last century, one Lady Lakeham was carted off to an asylum. Then there was a murder-suicide and a ghost and, well, Percy enjoys all that sort of thing, but I'm not sure we should indulge it. All this stuff with Anne Pargeter being sent for execution has left him a little bit obsessed with the dark side of life.

I don't know anything about the domestic arrangements such as who slept where or why. Is it important for anyone to know this? When Percy gets a wife it will be her problem, not his.

Ah, I remember we weren't allowed in the upper part of the house. This turned out to be a bit inconvenient for me as I needed somewhere to keep my pottery and Celia does get so annoyed with artefacts littering the place.

"I'm never sure if I've broken a five-thousand year old vase or a new one," she always says. "So do make life easier for me by keeping the five-thousand year old vases as far away from me as possible." I can't deny that life would be easier if she didn't break any vases, but she does seem to have a problem knowing where to put her arms and legs. Anne Pargeter was very helpful in that quarter. More than once, she managed a pretty good save whenever my wife floated past something and knocked it off its perch. She'd have made a good fielder for England. Anne, I mean, not Celia.

I didn't see Percy and Lily after lunch that first day. I think they had their tea up in the nursery. Sometime later that day, Bunty Lemington-Smith arrived for dinner. She was that old school friend of Celia's. I'd never liked her and I would like to say I was sorry about what happened to her, but I can't. There are things about her... Things that have happened...that make me feel she was a very

21

unpleasant woman.

No, hang on. That wasn't on the first day was it? Odd how all these experiences bunch up together, so that it's hard to recall what happened when. No, Bunty arrived a day or two later with Captain Marsh.

Something else happened that first day. Or rather that night. I had to go out to meet Sergei and Ivan, my contacts in the archaeology world. They had just brought back some new pottery for me. Well, it's old pottery, but new to me. We met in a pub in the village. I wasn't sure at first about letting Sergei and Ivan come up to the house. They were foreigners and foreigners aren't much liked or trusted in Britain since the war. They're both good sorts but I wasn't sure Celia would like it. Besides, the less people they met, the better.

They had some rather fine black pottery, from the very early Etruscan era, and I gladly bought it from them. Some of the pots will make marvellous illustrations for my book and the rest will go to museums. We had a few pints of beer, and a good chat about the dig they'd been on. I do miss those days, but with the restriction on travel in Eastern Europe now that the Iron Curtain has gone up, it'll be a while before I'm able to go again.

I was on my way back, rather late, and, I think, walking under the East wing when I heard the scream from one of the bedroom windows. I thought someone was being murdered. I rushed up to those rooms and I found Anne Pargeter in the corridor, being comforted by Maudie (I think she was the cook). Miss Pargeter claimed she'd had a nightmare, but a few days later that nightmare became a ghost. It's difficult to trust someone who changes their story like that.

Doctor Stanley Aitken

Anne Pargeter? Yes, she was an efficient enough young woman. She reminded me a bit of a spectator of a play. As if she was outside all of us, looking in. But she had one of those inscrutable faces and it was hard to know what she was thinking. Oh, she smiled often enough and said all the right things, but I never got a sense of really knowing the girl. She was a servant, after all, and one hardly notices them unless they break something in your presence. It was only later I realised I knew her, and by then it was too late.

It has been suggested that I arrived the same day as the Group Captain and Bunty Lemington-Smith, but I'm sure that's not correct. Let me check my diary…

Group Captain Guy Marsh

Here we are again. My testimony for my friend, Hotspur. I know I said I wasn't going to do this, but I had lunch with Celia Sullivan the other day. She seems to think I should be more helpful to her son in his quest for the truth, even if it does hurt him. So I'll indulge him for his mother's sake. There are some subjects that are out of bounds, but I suppose I can indicate when they arise.

Hotspur must be prepared for the truth to hurt. It certainly hurt me and I don't know if I will ever truly recover. But he is young, and his heart will heal over time.

The Sullivans had been at Lakeham Abbey a few days before I arrived. Hotspur and Anne Pargeter were already great friends by then and I think I was a bit of a gooseberry. Two's company, three's a crowd and all that.

I had brought Bunty Lemington-Smith with me. So it was four's a crowd. In fact, that woman had such a strange and noisy personality, she was a crowd all on her own. I won't bore you with the trip on the plane. Suffice to say that she and the engine vied for supremacy.

I landed my plane in the clearing in the plantation, and Anne and Hotspur come out to meet us. It was the first time I'd seen him let anyone but his attendant push his wheelchair. Henry was off relaxing somewhere, and I think little Lily was down for her afternoon nap.

23

I must say it felt good to receive such a warm welcome from both. I wasn't sure of the reception I'd get, as I'd more or less invited myself to stay, for reasons I think it's best not to go into.

When one lives in a tiny flat in bombed-out London, it's nice to stay in the country. Even if that country is the one that has let us all down since the war. We were promised a better world. Instead we came back to no jobs and a London totally obliterated.

I'm getting maudlin again, and none of this is Hotspur's fault. She did this to me. She did it to Hotspur too, which is why I'm not sure he should be trying to help her. He's a good lad, with a good heart, but his quest to save the damsel locked in the tower is a waste of time.

I remember the first time I saw her. As I said, she was pushing his wheelchair across the grass, towards the plane. He was You were waving like mad.

"Uncle Guy!"

"Hello, Hotspur!"

I'm not really his uncle. We're cousins or something, on his father's side. On his mother's side too. Upper class British families are a bit like that. We're all related to each other in some way. I have to admit I was more interested in Anne at that moment. I'd never met a woman quite like her. She was dressed all in black, but with a pristine white collar. Her white blonde hair was pinned back, and she had that frank, open expression that suggested she would never lie to you. We all got that wrong! But on that first day, she resembled a Madonna.

Perhaps that's a bit too biblical for what I was really feeling. She was so... Remember me saying that some things are out of bounds? My reaction to Anne is one of those things.

"Hotspur?" she said, raising her eyebrows.

"He always calls me that," Percy said, sighing. I think he liked it really. "My full name is Henry Percy Sullivan, but no one calls me by my first name. It would be confusing anyway, what with Henry, my attendant. Anyway, the nickname is Uncle Guy's idea of a joke. Sir Henry Percy was a medieval knight and everyone called him Hotspur."

"He was also one of the most valiant knights of his time," Anne said, smiling at me and then at the boy. "So I can see why the Group Captain thought of it."

I think he grew a few inches taller in that wheelchair and he didn't seem to mind the nickname so much after that.

"And how is Percy today?" Bunty Lemington-Smith asked. I realised she was talking to Anne rather than him. To be honest, I'd forgotten she was there and she'd been uncharacteristically quiet since we landed. I got the impression that she was also quite taken with Anne, because she couldn't keep her eyes off her.

"Percy is very well," he said. "But I am sitting down here in this bloody wheelchair, not up there."

Bunty did not even notice. Or perhaps she just did not care. "You must introduce yourself, you lovely creature," she said to Anne.

I think I might have showed off a bit after the introductions. "It's a Lancaster," I said, pointing to my plane, even though Anne had not asked the question. "My own. I bought it from old Air Force stock. Been helping out with the Berlin Airlift. One has to do what one can in these troubled times…"

I saw Bunty's lips twist into a wry grin. "Oh, we do," she said.

What a total fool I must have sounded to Anne, preening about my mission of mercy. I wanted her to be impressed with me. Perhaps that's something I don't have to explain to anyone who met her. She had that effect on everyone. We all wanted Anne Pargeter to think of us as handsome or efficient or capable. That was probably down to her Madonna effect, and we all worshipped her that summer.

"Oh yes," she agreed with me. "I do feel for people,

25

imprisoned behind that iron curtain. It makes you wonder what we fought for in the war."

"It's not actually a curtain or made of iron," Hotspur informed us all. "It's simply an impenetrable barrier, blocking east from west. The term Iron Curtain was first used by Ethel Snowdon in her book *Through Bolshevik Russia*, and then again in nineteen thirty-three by…"

On the way back to the house, he told us lots of very interesting facts about the Iron Curtain, but I can't quite remember them all. Young Hotspur was like that: a walking encyclopaedia. I suppose he has a lot of time to read up on facts, stuck in that wheelchair and unable to get out and run about like other boys.

"Mrs Sullivan is resting," Anne told me when Hotspur had exhausted his knowledge of all things Russia. "And Professor Sullivan is working on his pottery. We're just about to have lemonade and tea cakes on the terrace, if you'd like to join us, Miss Lemington-Smith? Group Captain?"

"Please, call me Guy."

"Guy it is…"

As we walked around to the terrace, I saw Bunty move closer to Anne and mutter something to her. Anne's already pale face became paler, and she shook her head vigorously. "No, I don't think so. I probably just have one of those faces." It was one of the first lies I heard her tell, but I didn't know it at the time.

"It's a very lovely face," Bunty said. "Like a film star." Anne faltered then and nearly tripped over behind Hotspur's wheelchair. I think she only stayed upright because she was holding onto it.

"Doctor Aitken!" Hotspur called, as we rounded the corner and saw a man standing there. He was looking down at the jug of lemonade and pile of teacakes with a perplexed expression on his face.

"Why, hello, lad."

"I'm sorry, Doctor Aitken," said Anne. "We had no idea you were arriving today."

"And you are?" He held out his hand to her.

"Anne Pargeter. I'm Mrs Sullivan's housekeeper for the summer. Where is your luggage, Doctor Aitken? I'll have it taken to your room."

"It's in my car. I'll get it in a while." The doctor waved her away. I got the impression he was not as enamoured of Anne as the rest of us. "Bunty, dear girl, what a nice surprise."

He kissed Bunty on the cheek. "And Group Captain Marsh? What brings you to these parts?"

"Bunty needed a lift and I sort of invited myself along."

"Still writing dodgy prescriptions, Doctor?" Bunty said.

"You're a card," Doctor Aitken replied, his smile looking rather fixed to me.

Then Celia and Freddie turned up and Anne brought Lily down, and we all sat down to lemonade and teacakes on the terrace. It was all so very normal and British.

"It's so good to see you, Guy," Celia said. She didn't seem to mind me just turning up.

"Don't you have important air-lifting to do?" Freddie asked. I don't think he was quite as pleased. I don't know why, as I've always liked Freddie, and I thought we got on well. I remembered that I had invited myself along and wondered if this was why he was a little cooler with me than usual.

I will say that Anne was always very clever. Even though she really was the one to preside over the table that afternoon, she had a way of letting Celia think she was in charge.

"Would you like to hold Lily?" Anne asked. She had Lily rested on one hip whilst balancing a plate of teacakes in her hand.

"I wouldn't let Celia do it," Bunty said. "She's liable to drop her."

"I'm sure she'll do no such thing," said Anne.

"Perhaps you'd like to pour the lemonade?"

"Would you do it please, Anne? Bunty is right. I'll probably drop her." I sometimes think Celia is afraid of small children. Or perhaps just her own. I know that Doctor Aitken had been treating her for nerves, and she appeared most nervous when with Hotspur and young Lily.

"Do try not to drop the jug," Bunty said. "It's probably worth more than the child."

"You are cruel sometimes, Bunty."

"Someone has to be, darling," Bunty replied. "Freddie lets you get away with too much. You used to be much cleverer. Motherhood has killed off your brain cells."

"Bunty!"

"Oh, you know I don't mean half of what I say, darling. Here, Miss Pargeter, let me hold the child."

"No!" Celia's voice made us all jump. "No, Bunty, you just enjoy your teacakes."

I saw Anne bite her lip, as she watched the exchange. She and I looked at each other, and we both appeared to understand what was happening there.

"I'm always a good mother when no one else is around," Celia said. For a moment I thought she would cry.

"You mean like when you left her in Harrods?" Bunty said.

"It's not uncommon," Anne said quietly. "When young mothers are busy and rushed."

I have to admit that I didn't much like Bunty Lemington-Smith. Anne took Lily as far from Bunty as she could reasonably get and I had a strange feeling she was punishing the woman.

"Tell us about your mother, Anne," Bunty said, having forgotten about Lily.

"She died many years ago," Anne replied, with a tight smile.

"Who was she? Where are your family from? Are you one of the Devon Pargeters?"

"I cannot claim such exalted relations," Anne replied. "My mother was in service, just as I am."

"Yet you've done well for yourself, working your way to such a high position. Sought after by most of the women in society and at a hefty price, too. How does that happen?"

Everyone around the table flinched. It's not the done thing in polite society to discuss a person's salary.

"There's no mystery," Anne said. "I give people what they want. And what most housewives want is not to have to worry about the petty little matters of running a home. So I take care of all that for them. And I do believe that women, as well as men, should be paid what they are worth."

"Anne has certainly been worth every penny so far," Celia said. "I feel so relaxed. Anyway, Bunty, you are being unkind when it was you who recommended her."

"I hadn't actually met her then. I'd only heard about her."

Anne laughed, but I saw worry behind her eyes. "Oh dear. Are you going to un-recommend me, Miss Lemington-Smith?"

"You remind me of someone," Bunty said. "I can't put my finger on it, but I know that face."

The conversation turned to films, and what was on at the cinema in the local town.

"I'm rather tired of war films," Celia said. "I'd like to see a nice romance. Not *Gone with the Wind*. I think I'm over Rhett Butler. They say Clark Gable had bad breath. What was that film we went to see when we were courting, Freddie? I'm sure it was the night you asked me to marry you."

"Don't ask me," said Freddie in lazy tones. "I think I fell asleep."

"That sounds about right," said Bunty.

"I hope you awoke for the proposal," Anne quipped. She stood up, with Lily resting on one hip, and started to deftly pour out more lemonade for everyone, passing around the glasses.

"Oh, I remember." I don't think Celia had been listening to what the others said. She was wrapped up in her memories. "It was called *The Heart Knows,* and starred Eleanor Grace. She was incredibly beautiful. It's so tragic, the way she killed herself…"

I'm not sure what happened then, only that I heard a gasp and my trousers were suddenly drenched with lemonade. One of the glasses was broken in pieces on the terrace floor. I looked up to see Anne, standing above me, impassive and inscrutable, before she bent over to pick up the broken glass, whilst still balancing Lily on one hip.

Young Hotspur, who had appeared bored with the conversation, piped up, "Anne, tell everyone about the ghost."

Doctor Stanley Aitken

Now I come to think of it, I do recall the lemonade and tea cakes on the terrace, and someone breaking a glass. I think it was Anne Pargeter who dropped it, which was a surprise as she had been sold to us all as a paragon of household virtue.

I also remember Mrs Sullivan and Miss Lemington-Smith having an argument later that day. I didn't mean to eavesdrop. I'd simply taken my suitcase upstairs and was making my way back along the corridor nearest to Celia's sitting room when I heard them talking.

"Why do you always put me down, Bunty?" Celia was asking.

"What do you mean, Celia?"

"You always have something to say about my mothering or housekeeping skills, and it's always bad."

"Don't be a fool, Celia. I can't help it if you're not meant for the domestic realm."

"I think I've been a very good wife to Freddie. And I'm the best mother I can be."

"That's not saying much."

"People who have never had children always claim to be experts on their upbringing! I seem to recall that you also forgot that Lily was in Harrods."

"She's not my responsibility."

"No, and neither was Percy…" Celia said something else, but I couldn't make it out.

"What's that supposed to mean?"

I think I might have stepped on a creaky floorboard, because Celia stammered "N…nothing. Forget it. Let's just try and have a nice, peaceful dinner without you picking on everyone's faults."

"You know that everything I say, I say for your own good, don't you, Celia?" Bunty said. "You asked me, many years ago to make sure you didn't do anything wrong."

I didn't hear the reply. I don't know what was going on, only that it seemed that Bunty Lemington-Smith wasn't that much of a friend and dear Celia might have resented her for some reason.

As for the ghost, it was a load of stuff and nonsense; a way of Miss Pargeter getting attention for herself. If you ask me, the girl had a flair for the dramatic. It's hardly surprising, knowing what we know now.

Anne Pargeter

Dearest Hotspur, you're not going to give up on your friend Anne, are you? Both your mother and Group Captain Marsh have written to me in the last few days. I can't tell you what I thought, seeing both their letters amongst my mail. I read your mother's and almost ripped up the Group Captain's. He hasn't contacted me since the day I was arrested. Curiosity got the better of me.

Your mother simply asked me to help you in your investigation. It was a very kind note, under the circumstances, but your mother is a very kind woman. The Group Captain's letter asked if he might visit me in prison. He said I was to agree for your sake and yours alone. As reluctant as I was to see him after all that had occurred, I could not refuse such a request.

It was a dull, cold day when they took me down to see him. I had seen no other visitors, apart from my legal counsel, in all the time I had been in prison. But there I was, face to face with him. Despite everything, we met as virtual strangers.

The first time I saw Guy Marsh, it had been a sunny day and he had just landed his Lancaster in front of the Abbey. Do you remember? He had brought Bunty Lemington-Smith with him. I suppose I should not say this under the circumstances, but she truly was ghastly and made so many people unhappy.

On that day, I only had eyes for him. Not just because I'd never met such a handsome man but also because there was something familiar about him. It dredged up some part of the past that I had hoped to bury. His touchingly diffident boasting about taking part in the Berlin Air Lift set him apart from any other man I'd known. I wanted to impress him as much as he seemed to want to impress me.

When we met face to face in the prison, that shy man had gone and the warmth in his chestnut brown eyes was replaced by a cold, hard glare.

I must have looked very different to him, with my prison pallor and my dyed blonde hair grown out to its original auburn. I daresay it only reminded him of my deceit.

"Understand I come only for our young friend, Hotspur," he said.

"I do understand." Even as I spoke the words I wished he would take me in his arms and tell me that he loved me. I wanted this even though I knew he was not allowed to touch me anyway.

"He wants to get the bottom of this…this business. His mother and father are worried about him."

"I worry about him too," I said. I wanted to weep but I have held back the tears for so long I think I have

32

forgotten how to. It is the only way to survive in this place. Tears mean weakness and one cannot show that here.

"Do you?" His words snapped out. "It's hard to tell with you, Anne. You've told so many lies." He scoffed. "I don't even know what to call you anymore. Is it Anne? Is it Mary-Ann?"

"I daresay it doesn't really matter," I said with as much dignity as I could muster. "What…what do you want me to do for Percy?"

"Make him understand that you're meant to be here and that you're meant to die. He doesn't believe it. Not really. To him, you're like one of the cowboys or soldiers he sees in the cinema who die in one film only to reappear as someone else in the next feature. You must make him see that's not going to happen."

"How am I supposed to do that?"

"Tell him the truth, for God's sake!"

"I've already told the truth." That was, in fact, a lie. I hadn't told the truth at all.

If only he had seen through my lies, it would have made this ordeal easier, because I would have had his love to sustain me through what is to come. His willingness to believe the very worst of me has left me mired in darkness and I have no strength left to fight.

There was little for us to say to each other after that. He asked if they were treating me well. I said they were. He asked if I'd been given a date for my execution yet. I said yes, and told him what date it would be. We might have been two strangers meeting at a cocktail party, had the subject matter not been so macabre. Then he said goodbye and I was taken back to my cell.

You, my dear Hotspur, are my only friend now and because of that I owe it to you to set down my own version of events. I can only tell you the truth, even if no one else believes me.

I was so happy at Lakeham Abbey, those first few days. I think we all were. There was some tension, with

33

Bunty Lemington-Smith, but it did not really seem to matter.

I do not wish to speak ill of the woman (yet I seem to be managing to do so quite well), but I believe that Bunty's presence made your mother unhappy. I gather they had been friends at school and I also suspect, from things I overheard, that your mother's marriage made Bunty dreadfully sad. As a result, I think she wanted to make your mother miserable, by undermining her at every turn.

In this job I do – the job I did – I always made a point of letting the lady of the house know that she was the lady of the house. I always deferred to her, even if I did not always agree with what she did. Well, let's say I was good at pretending to defer to the lady of the house, whilst getting my own way. Does that sound rather Machiavellian of me? I'm afraid it does. But I would never suggest that a woman was bad for her children or her husband. The reason I took up the role I did was because I wanted to make families happy. My own family life had been miserable, for all the reasons that have come out in the press. All I ever wanted was to undo that wrong, by making others happy.

Believe me when I say that your mother is the very best of women, and if one who claimed to be her friend had not abused her so much, she would be a more serene wife and mother. Some people are toxic and I'm afraid Miss Lemington-Smith was one of those people.

Where shall I start my story? I cannot yet bring myself to talk about the events of my childhood. I know that the prison warders read everything I write, and I do not want my words twisted and used against me.

As you know I was at Lakeham Abbey several days before you all arrived. I hired my old friend, Maudie, to cook. Did I ever tell you that she was our cook when I was a child? Like your attendant, Henry, she doesn't say much, but as you are aware she prepares wonderful meals. She also knows how to get hold of the ingredients for those meals, if you know what I mean (I shan't say any more than that, what with the warders checking my letters).

Then you arrived. I can't say that I knew we would be friends straight away. I must admit that I saw you then as a tired and grumpy little boy who was fed up that no one spoke directly to him. I wasn't even sure we should like each other. I am so glad we got to know each other better and became firm friends. Even if you do have a tendency to swear at people when you're tired and grumpy!

Nothing much had happened at the Abbey until that night. It was quite a spooky place and I daresay I made a fuss over nothing.

I know I'd gone to bed glad that I'd made a new friend and that everyone had settled in so well. I may have appeared calm and collected on the surface, but in reality I was a bag of nerves, terrified that things would go wrong and that your parents would dismiss me immediately. I collapsed onto my bed, without undressing, and began to doze off.

The East wing of Lakeham Abbey is not as well looked after as the West wing, hence the servants were living on that side. We had cleared the rooms and swept the floors as best we could, but some grime is so ingrained, it never goes away. We dared not wash the drapes in case they fell apart. The blankets and bedspreads were paper thin, so we put those away and replaced them with newer bedding from the unused rooms in the West wing. I reasoned that if your parents had extra guests I'd have to pop into town and get some new linen.

None of us minded our surroundings. The rooms were still larger and more comfortable than the average servants' quarters. As we spent little time there, other than to sleep, it did not matter anyway. Everything was old and decrepit, and it gave the East wing a very 'Miss Havisham' air. I often expected her to appear at any moment.

Perhaps this was on my mind as I dozed, but I was also thinking of my mother. She had been in my thoughts a lot since I had arrived at Lakeham Abbey. At some point, I became aware of my bedroom door opening and someone – a figure in a hooded cloak – gliding across the room towards me. At the time I did not know if I was asleep and dreaming or half-wake and half-dreaming, or whether it was all absolutely real. It was both real and unreal, as is the way of dreams, yet I was also aware of a draught from the window and the rather lumpy bed beneath me.

She drew closer and closer, but her face was in shadow, so I could not see who she was.

My voice was constricted and I could move neither my arms nor legs. She put her hand on my cheek and stroked it. "Little girl must sleep," she whispered.

I think that was when I screamed…

Percy Sullivan

I saw the ghost too, but that was much later, and this story is starting to get all mixed up as it is so I'll save it for later. Anne saw the ghost before the Group Captain and Bunty Lemington-Smith arrived, and before the doctor arrived.

I wonder what the conversation between Mummy and Bunty was really about. I didn't like Bunty but I'm sorry for what happened. That's the sort of thing grown-ups say when they're not really upset so I suppose I must be growing up now. She never looked me in the eye, and hardly ever spoke to me directly. Even the doctor was capable of talking straight to me, but I suppose he works with sick people all the time.

What I don't understand is why Father's friends need to go to Eastern Europe to dig for Etruscan pottery when it can be found in Italy. Its proper name is Bucchero (derived from the Latin *poculum*). It's pre-Roman and because of the iron oxide in the pottery, it changes from red to black when fired in the kiln. For pottery that dates back to before Roman times, Father and his friends seemed to find an awful lot of it over the summer at Lakeham Abbey.

I remember Sergei and Ivan. I liked them even though I didn't see them often. They were like a couple of Cossacks. I think Mummy was a bit bemused by them when they came to dinner one night. Bunty didn't like them at all. Anne served them goulash. I'd never had it, and was a bit put out at not being able to join everyone for dinner, so the next day she let us eat the leftovers for our nursery tea. I was a bit disappointed that it was only red stew, but it was quite tasty.

Anne always knew how to make people happy with food. Mummy does her best and Maudie works for us now (that was my idea because she had nowhere else to go), but it's not the same as having Anne there to help serve it. She would always talk to me and Lily about where our food came from. She said it was important to know. Like when she told us that tinned corned beef comes from South America and all about the Welsh speaking Patagonians in Argentina.

I don't have enough information yet to draw conclusions (deductions, assumptions) about the murders. If Anne were here she'd probably be able to work it all out. Girls are stupid as a rule, but she's very clever. Though Father said she's not that clever if she's been convicted of murder. I tried to explain to him: "Father, she's a patsy."

"A what?"

"A patsy. Like in the gangster films." Father doesn't watch many films so I had to get my thesaurus out. "A pawn, a sucker…"

"Anne Pargeter is no one's fool, Percy. You'd do well to remember that."

I don't know why I bother…

I must get more evidence, but I don't know how. I wonder if Mother would let Henry take me back to Lakeham Abbey for a few days. No one lives there, so we wouldn't be in the way.

I hope Jennifer doesn't think she's going to steal this investigation away from me. She's rather bossy that way.

Celia Sullivan

I can't really explain about an argument between Bunty and myself. I'm sure the doctor was wrong, as none of it sounds like anything we would say to each other. There's something not quite nice about listening at bedroom doors and I'm surprised the doctor not only did it, but also admitted to Percy that he had. I'm sure he meant well, but he's got it all wrong.

Anne's ghost did appear to her before Bunty and Group Captain Marsh arrived. It was all very strange, as she didn't seem to be a fanciful sort of girl. She was really rather sensible. Those old houses do have an effect on one. For a few nights afterwards, I was sure I heard footsteps above me, but Bunty said I was suggestible.

Freddie and Bunty did have a difference of opinion. We'd been at the Abbey a few weeks, and had invited some people over for dinner. I think that Sergei and Ivan were there and we had goulash, which was actually very nice. They've never got on, Freddie and Bunty. I always used to wish they would, as she was my best friend at school, and Freddie was…is…the love of my life. I could never get them to be friends, no matter how hard I tried.

Sergei and Ivan seemed to be very pleasant men, though neither spoke English very well. It's lucky that Freddie knows some Hungarian. I do remember how very hungry they looked and that they seemed to eat their meals very carefully, as if they were afraid of showing themselves up. I don't suppose they'd eaten in a grand house before. One of the men – Sergei, I think – was wearing a shirt with frayed sleeves. At one point during dinner, the sleeve rolled up a little and I saw that he had a tattoo on his wrist. I presumed he was from the circus or something. I'm sure that he was a nice person, but it did surprise me that Freddie should make friends with circus folk.

Bunty was teasing me in her usual manner. I'm sure she never meant anything by it. She had always been that way. Well, not always. When we were at school, she was a sweet girl and my very best friend. We used to have such fun. Once we put a frog in old Mrs Partridge's drawer, and she screamed blue murder! Things were fun back then. The Great War was over, and we had no idea there would be another one.

Then we left school and had our 'coming out'. Bunty was the dearest of girls, but she was never very pretty. Is it big-headed to say that I was rather nice to look at? Well, big-headed or not, it was true. So I got lots of attention from young men, but she didn't.

I could have married several times before I met Freddie. I had lots of offers. But none of them ever followed through. It was as if they started off liking me well enough, but suddenly went cold. Bunty always knew. She'd say as soon as I met a young man, "He won't stick around long. He doesn't really love you." She was always right. They went away soon afterwards.

Freddie Sullivan moved with a different crowd to ours. They were older and more intellectual than my usual set. We met at a friend's house party one summer. In fact now I come to think of it, it was the Carstairs. Emma and Angus had only recently married, and she had just been told that Jennifer was on the way.

Bunty wasn't there. She'd had to go to hospital to have her appendix out and it was taking her a while to heal. I wasn't allowed to visit her for some reason. I never really found out why. It was strange to be without her, but I was determined to make the best of it.

I thought Freddie was so sweet, with his limp and his pipe and his floppy hair that was never quite tidy. He never expected too much of me, and seemed to just like it that I listened to him. I must admit I didn't understand a lot of what he was saying, but perhaps he thought I was being reflective and didn't realise until it was too late that I'm really rather stupid. I did like listening to his voice and if I fell asleep it certainly wasn't boredom but because he spoke so softly and I relaxed around him.

We'd only been going out for a few weeks– we went to the pictures to see Eleanor Grace in *The Heart Knows* – such a wonderful film – and afterwards, as we walked along the embankment in London, he said to me, "I didn't think much of the film. It was a bit too melodramatic for my liking, but I think the title is accurate. My heart knows that I've found the woman I want to spend the rest of my life with. Will you marry me, Celia?"

"Can we marry quickly?" I asked, feeling a sudden sense of urgency. "Because if we don't, you'll go off me and I don't know what I shall do then."

He kissed me and promised me that he would never go off me, but we married by special licence the next day anyway (Freddie told the registrar that he was going off on a dig in the Middle East, and couldn't take me unless I was his wife). Emma and Angus Carstairs were our witnesses.

Bunty was very upset when she found out, and sent me a rather nasty letter about it all. I suppose because we didn't invite her. There was hardly time for that. Even our parents didn't come to the wedding, but my mother was very happy for us.

"Best thing that could have happened," Mother said. I think she was relieved as I was already twenty-two and almost in danger of being left on the shelf.

I didn't see Bunty for several months, because as soon as we married, we did go off on that dig in the Middle East. I was happy there. Everyone treated me so politely and didn't mind that I didn't always understand what was going on. In fact, I got quite good at cataloguing the pottery that they found each day. Freddie said I had the nicest writing he'd ever seen. Then I found out that Percy was on the way, and we came home so that I could have him in a nice, clean hospital with no mosquitoes.

Anyway, for whatever reason, perhaps because we didn't give her a chance to be bridesmaid at our wedding and then we went away for so long, Bunty and my husband never did get on very well. It was a pity as I loved them both and wished they'd be friends.

She came around eventually, when Percy was about a year old, and even helped me to take care of him…

I'm so sorry. Someone came to the door whilst I was writing and I seem to have lost where I was. Oh yes. Freddie and Bunty's argument.

We were at dinner, eating the red stew with Sergei and Ivan, and Bunty was teasing Freddie about Anne Pargeter. Actually, we'd finished the stew. Anne had left the room to fetch dessert.

"She's a bit too pretty, if you ask me," Bunty had said. "Though I daresay you like having her around, Freddie. How long have you and Celia been married now? Fourteen years? You're well past the seven-year itch. You want to watch him, Celia."

It had not occurred to me until that moment that Freddie might be attracted to Anne, but I must admit to feeling worried when Bunty put it into words. Anne was younger and far more intelligent than I was. I had liked her until then, but I began to wonder if she would make a much better wife for a very clever professor.

"Celia and I have survived a lot," Freddie said, glaring at her. "A pretty girl who just happens along is not going to break up our marriage."

Sergei and Ivan seemed a bit confused. Freddie said something to them in Hungarian and they smiled and nodded, as if they understood. I wish I'd known what he said, and must admit I was afraid he'd told them he was in love with Anne. I realised straight away that was silly of me. Even in a foreign language, Freddie wouldn't humiliate me to other men. If he truly planned to break my heart into tiny pieces he would be a perfect gentleman about it.

"What about the Group Captain?" asked Bunty. I can't remember where Guy was that night. He'd gone somewhere, saying he had to see someone. Doctor Aitken had also left to visit an old patient who lived in the neighbourhood. "Guy's a very handsome, heroic sort, flying off around the world. Must hurt you, Freddie, with that club foot of yours."

"It won't work, Bunty," said Freddie, but I saw doubt behind his eyes. "Try as you might, it won't work. It might have, with all those other fools who were in love with Celia and couldn't go the distance, but I'm made of stronger stuff."

She scoffed at that.

"This is silly," I said. "Why are you both teasing each other so much? It's not even amusing." It was disturbing and even though Sergei and Ivan might not have understood much of what we were saying, I was afraid they'd go away with a bad opinion of us. I'm not very good with atmospheres and things like that, but I do believe there was something in the air that night.

"There's something about that Anne Pargeter," Bunty said. "Something devious. And I aim to find out what it is."

Anne came back into the room as Bunty spoke.

"Leave it alone, Bunty," Freddie said.

"Would anyone like Pavlova?" Anne asked in her cheery way. "With fresh raspberries?" She set the dessert down in the middle of the table. It looked magnificent, with its bright white meringue and blood red raspberries.

Sergei and Ivan nodded readily, and she served them first. We ate it in silence, and then both Guy and the doctor returned. Anne served them – she had saved them some of the red stew and I must admit I cursed her efficiency – and we all made small talk. Guy spoke Hungarian too, so was able to involve Sergei and Ivan. Unfortunately, that left the rest of us out.

"You may leave us, Anne," I said, rather sharply. I couldn't help wondering if Freddie was looking at her all the time. He might not have bothered before, but perhaps Bunty's words had put ideas in his head.

"Of course, Mrs Sullivan. Would you like any tea or coffee?"

"I can manage that. You may leave us."

Anne looked a little hurt then, but I was in no mood to placate her. I was happy at Lakeham Abbey that summer. Or I had been to begin with. In fact, I was even after what happened with Bunty, but on that night there seemed to be a poisonous pall over the room and I thought Anne was responsible for it. I realise now how foolish I've been and for so many years. As I said, I'm not good with atmospheres and what might cause them.

"I aim to find out her secret," Bunty said when Anne had gone. "There's something going on here. I wanted to go to one of the upper floors earlier and she stopped me. Said the doors were locked. I wonder what she's hiding up there."

"A ghost, probably," Doctor Aitken joked, and when Freddie had explained everything to Sergei and Ivan, we all laughed. Well, all of us except Guy. I got the feeling he was a little perplexed about the whole thing, even though he had heard the story of Anne's ghostly apparition.

The following day the Carstairs arrived. Their daughter, Jennifer is a beautiful girl. All flowing hair and long legs.

"You'll be able to play with Percy," I suggested, as Anne and I showed them to their rooms.

"I'm too old to play." Jennifer sniffed.

"Ignore her, Celia," Emma Carstairs said. "She's at that age where she'll argue black is white if it's the opposite of what you think."

"I am not," Jennifer said, flouncing off ahead. "Anyway, what can I play with a boy in a wheelchair? We can hardly go climbing trees."

"Board games?" Anne suggested.

"Boring."

Emma and I exchanged knowing glances. We both knew what it was to have a prepubescent child in the house. Percy could be just as contrary.

After we settled them into their rooms, Anne took Jennifer off to meet Percy and Lily, whilst Emma and I had a cup of tea. Angus and Freddie had disappeared into Freddie's office, talking men stuff.

"How are you, Celia?" asked Emma. "I must say you cope so well with Percy."

"I… Yes, I suppose I do," I said. In truth, Henry and Anne were the ones who really coped with Percy and his various needs and moods, but I was happy to take the credit.

"I didn't realise there was tea," said Bunty from the door. "No one informed me." She had a dark look on her face. It was one I'd seen before.

"Sorry, Bunty. I thought you were out exploring the village. What can I get you?"

"Nothing. I'm not bothered now."

"Goodness, you sound just like my Jennifer." Emma laughed. "Aren't you a bit too old for sulking, Bunty?"

It's fair to say that Emma and Bunty had never much liked each other either. We had been at the same school, but at the time, Emma had moved in different circles. She was the intellectual type.

"Aren't you a bit too old for that dress, Emma?" Bunty asked.

"It's a Chanel, Bunty. I don't expect you to know that. You buy your clothes at the army and navy stores, don't you?"

"Now, girls," I said, trying to laugh, but feeling my throat constricting. I hated these scenes, despite Emma being perfectly capable of holding her own with Bunty. I wanted to tell her that if she carried on, I would be the one to suffer, but that seemed rather melodramatic. "Let's play nicely."

"How is Angus?" asked Bunty, sitting down and taking a slice of fruit cake from the coffee table. She bit into it, and for a moment her teeth looked like some sort of predator. "Still working with Mildred?"

"Mildred is a very fine secretary."

"I've heard he thinks so."

There had been rumours in the lesser newspapers about Angus and his secretary for some time, but he had dismissed it all as rubbish. He would not be the first Member of Parliament to have an affair with his parliamentary secretary, but he was considered up and coming, and it was rumoured he would soon be offered a ministry. Any sort of scandal would put a stop to that.

"Of course he thinks so," Emma responded, looking strained. "Angus is a man who gives credit where it's due."

"Tell me about your dress, Emma," I cut in. "Did you get it when you were in Paris? I imagined all the salons were bombed out."

Bunty sat fuming in the corner whilst Emma and I discussed fashion. I realise now it was wrong to leave Bunty out of things, but she could be so difficult at times. Eventually she got up and left the room.

"Darling Celia," Emma said. "Why on earth do you put up with that awful woman?"

"She's been my best friend since school."

"And your worst enemy," Emma said, pointedly.

Later that day, Bunty took me aside and said, "Why the hell did you invite her? You know I hate her."

"You hate everyone, Bunty," I said, sighing. "If I stopped inviting all the people you dislike, I should never see anyone else."

"Why should that matter? We're the true friends here. She doesn't even like you. She's just using you to get cheap accommodation until they find a house."

Dinner that night was another tense affair. I worried that Freddie spent most of his time looking at Anne. She did not join us for dinner, as we had guests, but she came in to help with the serving.

Angus Carstairs drank heavily. He was not yet fifty,

but his cheeks were florid and tiny red veins were breaking out on his nose.

As a treat we had allowed Percy and Jennifer to join us. It was Emma's idea, as Jennifer was often allowed to sit in on grown up dinner parties.

"Did you and Jennifer play some nice games?" I asked Percy.

"No."

"Why not?"

"She doesn't want to play with me."

"Oh," said Emma, glaring at her daughter. "I'm sure she does, don't you, Jennifer?"

"Not really." Jennifer shrugged. "I'm too old for games. And he's a real know-it-all."

"Jennifer!" Angus barked at her. "You are a guest in this house, and as such you will show some manners."

I felt sorry for the child then. Her eyes filled with tears and her hands started shaking. "Yes, Daddy. I'm sorry, Mrs Sullivan."

"And who else do you need to apologise to?"

"I'm sorry, Percy."

"It's alright, Jennifer," said Percy. I immediately sensed that my boy understood the situation. He's clever like that and gets atmospheres much better than I do. "You're right. Board games are boring. If I could run and climb trees I would, but I just can't."

"Won't your legs ever work?" Jennifer asked.

"No. I don't think so."

"I'm sure that if I were in a wheelchair I should try every day to walk again."

"It doesn't happen just like that," Percy snapped.

"We can find something to do, I'm sure." She did not sound sure, but she was a bit kinder to him after that.

"We could look for the ghost," Percy said.

"There's a ghost?" Jennifer's eyes lit up.

"Anne saw it. I'll tell you all about it before bedtime."

"Excellent!"

Once again Emma and I exchanged glances. I liked

having another mother there; particularly someone who understood how hard it could be to please a precocious child.

"It's all rubbish," said Bunty. Like Angus she had been steadily drinking. "That Anne is an attention seeker."

"You'd know about that," Angus said, taking another drink of wine.

I began to wonder if we should have rationed the alcohol.

"How is Mildred?" Bunty asked. "I thought I saw you and her together in Knightsbridge. Outside a hotel?"

"You did not," Angus said.

"One day someone will find pictures."

"Bunty, that's enough," I said. "Think of the children." Percy did not seem to be upset as much as interested, but I could see that the conversation was upsetting Jennifer.

"They're not mine," Bunty scoffed. "You're only worried that I'll start on Freddie's obsession with Anne again."

Freddie slammed his knife and fork down. "I do not have an obsession with Anne. You're the one with the obsession, Bunty. Now, if you continue to upset my guests, I'm going to have to ask you to leave."

"Celia invited me. Not you."

"Then Celia can un-invite you!"

"Just stop it!" I said, throwing down my napkin. "I'm tired of all this bickering. Can't we just have a nice, pleasant evening together?"

"Mother," Percy said, his eyes brimming over.

"Oh, it's alright, darling. Everything is alright. Isn't it, everyone? We're all just being silly and playing a game, aren't we? Aren't we?"

There were murmurs around the table, but dinner never quite got off the ground that night.

Freddie stayed in my room, because I was upset. He wanted to prove to me that he had no interest in Anne, and I must admit he did rather a good job of it. He left me feeling much more relaxed.

"What was that?" I said, when a scream tore through the night.

"I've no idea."

"It's probably Anne seeing her ghost again," I said. "I think Bunty is right about her doing it for attention." It's strange how quickly you could go off someone. Especially when you believe she's a rival for your husband's affections.

I'm ashamed to say that we fell asleep until the early morning.

It was about six o'clock when Freddie got up and went to the window and looked out.

"What the—" He swore, which is most unlike him.

"What is it, Freddie?" I asked.

"Stay where you are, darling. You don't need to see this."

I didn't listen to him, of course. I went to his side and looked out of the window. "On the terrace," he said. I looked across towards the terrace, which runs all the way across that side of the house to the East wing.

Lying on the ground with her arms and legs flailed out and her head at a sickening angle was Bunty Lemington-Smith.

Chapter Four

Group Captain Guy Marsh

I think I must have seen Bunty lying on the ground before Freddie and Celia. I know I was first onto the scene that morning, and I immediately called for Doctor Aitken, and made a mental note to get in touch with my stepbrother, Andrew, at Scotland Yard. Anne had followed me out, bringing a tray of tea things with her, presumably as we were going to have breakfast on the terrace. The memory that sticks with me to this day is that she didn't even drop the tray. She put it down on the table and came across to look, as if seeing a dead body on a patio was a regular occurrence. Then I noticed that her hands were shaking and I reassessed my judgement. My own were too. I still had dark memories of such an accident, even though I had not witnessed that event personally.

"Go and fetch the doctor," I told her, even though I knew it was too late. There were pieces of stone around the body, which gave me the odd sensation of Bunty being some wrongdoer who had been stoned to death. I doubted that was the case, even if it seemed she had upset nearly everyone in the house. "And call the police."

During the time Anne was away, Celia and Freddie came down. Celia was understandably in a state. I know she and Bunty had been very close. I presume the Carstairs were still in bed, sleeping.

"Her neck is broken," the doctor told us after he'd done a quick examination. "And judging by the position of her body, I'd say she fell from a great height."

We all instinctively looked up. I didn't know it then, but one of the windows above us was Anne's bedroom. It was the roof that caught our attention. Some of the balustrade had come loose, leaving a gap.

"She must have fallen from there," I suggested. Everyone agreed.

"Except that part of the house is locked off to us all," Anne said. I can only presume now that she was acting innocent when she knew exactly what had happened.

"Don't you have the keys, Miss Pargeter?" the doctor asked.

"I'm sorry, but no, I don't. We were warned when we arrived that it was out of bounds, due to the sorry state of the upstairs rooms. I suppose they must have known that the roof was dangerous too."

"There must be a way up there," said Doctor Aitken. "She probably went wandering during the night and lost her footing. Didn't I hear her speaking to you just after dinner, Miss Pargeter?"

"Yes, that's correct. She wanted to know more about the house." Even then, with the rose tinted glasses I had taken to wearing in Anne's presence, I sensed she was lying. But I honestly thought she had her own reasons, and there was nothing to suggest that Bunty's death was anything other than a tragic accident. "I told her that I didn't know much."

"She seemed quite irate about it," the doctor murmured.

"She was a very formidable woman," Anne said, adding quickly. "With all due respect."

"No, you're right," Freddie agreed. "If Bunty wanted something, she was quite forceful about it."

A few minutes later, Hotspur came around the corner, pushed by Henry.

"What's happened?"

"Take him away from here, Henry," Freddie ordered. "There's been an accident."

"Let me see!" He tried to propel his wheelchair

forward, but Henry held tight to the handles and wouldn't let him move. "Is it a crime? What's happened?" The kid was rather excited by it all, in the way the young are when they don't quite understand death.

"Percy, dear," Anne said, kneeling down in front of the wheelchair. Freddie, Doctor Aitken, and I formed a sort of barrier around Bunty's body. Celia sat on one of the chairs, sobbing. "It's your Aunt Bunty. She's had an accident. Now you mustn't look. It's very upsetting. Henry, take him away, please. I'll come and prepare your breakfast soon."

Henry did that, whilst Hotspur complained, insisting he didn't want any breakfast. "I want to see the dead bloody body!"

I got the impression that he didn't have much love for Bunty either.

The police came along and they decided that Bunty had suffered a fall after wandering into a part of the house that was unsafe. Oddly, they never did find out how she got up onto the roof, and with all the doors between the floors locked and bolted. They broke one of the doors down, to gain access to the roof, but found nothing other than a pile of cigarette butts of the type that Bunty smoked. The consensus was that she had been up there smoking – having found some secret passage – and accidentally stumbled against the stone balustrade, which then gave way.

I doubt any of us even considered that murder was involved, or that Anne was the culprit, especially as she had not met Bunty before we all arrived at the Abbey. Even Bunty's words at dinner, about finding out the truth about Anne, did not occur to any of us. Bunty was a very forceful woman, and if she got it into her head to do something, she did it, even if the reasons did not make sense.

Later, Doctor Aitken told a different story, about the argument between Anne and Bunty, but that was only when Anne was accused and it was clear he had no choice but to come forward.

Doctor Stanley Aitken

Of course I remember the argument now but at the time I didn't think it meant anything. I was as taken in by Miss Pargeter as everyone else was. Besides, what reason would she have to kill a woman she had only met a few weeks earlier?

In the interests of justice, I will set down that argument, as much as I remember it.

It happened in the library, just before we all went up for bed. I don't think the two women realised I was in there, as I sat in a window seat, behind the closed drapes. I am always very happy to be invited to house parties, but sometimes a man needs time alone, to reflect on all he has seen and heard. A man in my position needs to know about the people he is spending time with. I must say it had been a most interesting dinner and I had much on which to ruminate.

I heard someone come in and move around the room, I presume looking for a book to read. I just hoped I would not be disturbed by someone who wanted pleasant conversation with me. Then I heard door opened wider (I believe the hinges are in need of oiling) and someone else came in.

"I hoped I'd find you here." I closed my eyes. I found I could only deal with Miss Lemington-Smith in small doses. Thankfully she was not speaking to me.

"Is there anything I can get you, Miss Lemington-Smith?" That was Miss Pargeter. I realised then that she was the first person to enter the room.

"The truth about you would be a good start," said Miss Lemington-Smith.

"I'm not sure what you mean," said Miss Pargeter.

"I recognised you the moment I saw you. You're the image of her. Even with the hair dye and the pancake make-up. Which really doesn't suit you, you know."

"The image of whom?"

"Your mother."

"You knew my mother? That is hard to believe as you're not that much older than I and she died when I was a baby."

"I'm sure that's the story you tell everyone. Must be hard, having a known murderer for a mother."

"My mother was not a murderer. I think you have me mistaken for someone else." Miss Pargeter began to sound alarmed, clearly upset by Miss Lemington-Smith's accusations. I wished I could see her, to gauge the look on her face. Did she look guilty or innocent? But I dared not come out of my hiding place. I knew it would bring too quick an end to the conversation. "If we're going to talk about honesty," she began to say, "Let's talk about you and the way you undermine Mrs Sullivan at every opportunity."

"I don't know what you mean." It was Miss Lemington-Smith's turn to sound rattled.

"You put her down whenever you can, and it only increases her nervousness. I just cannot work out whether your jealousy is about her or about him."

"How dare you?"

"No, how dare you, Miss Lemington-Smith. Coming here accusing me of goodness knows what when your own motives for being here are very suspect. I will not let you upset Mrs Sullivan. I've become very fond of her and I am convinced that with the right support she can be a wonderful mother."

Miss Lemington-Smith barked with laughter. "Then you should ask her why Percy is in a wheelchair. I will find out the truth about you, Anne Pargeter, and then you'll be out of this house. I'll see to it myself that Celia dismisses you."

"So that you can continue to maintain a toxic influence on her life?"

"That was the wrong thing to say. You really should not have made an enemy of me, Miss Pargeter." I heard the door slam.

"Nor you of me," said Miss Pargeter to what she thought was an empty room.

That wasn't the only disagreement I heard that night. It seemed that Miss Lemington-Smith was determined to upset everyone in the house.

I was out on the terrace, smoking a cigarette, when I heard voices from an open window above me. I think it must have been in the East wing, so when I heard Miss Lemington-Smith, I did wonder what she was doing there.

"What are you creeping around for, Bunty?" I recognised the dulcet tones of Mrs Emma Carstairs.

"Mind your own business."

"I think it's you who should mind your own business, Bunty," Mrs Carstairs said. "You really cannot resist stirring things, can you?"

"About your husband and his mistress, you mean?"

"You won't win, no matter how hard you try. Angus and I are solid. Nothing will break us up. It hasn't in the past, and it won't now."

I think I heard Miss Lemington-Smith scoff. "Does he know that you only put up with his affairs because if he found out the truth about you, it might test his commitment to your marriage?"

"I'm not sure what you mean."

"Everyone knows how you used to run around before your marriage, Emma. You held a lot of young men under your spell. Not one of them worth a jot. Or a penny, for that matter. Then suddenly you marry a man nearly fifteen years older than yourself and less than seven months later, young Jennifer pops out."

"You clearly have your dates wrong," said Emma. "So if I were you, I'd be very careful about slinging that accusation. I love my husband and he, despite his problems, loves me. I know it's hard for you to see anyone happy, Bunty, especially Celia, but in the end we will all outlast you."

I thought of those words 'we will all outlast you', when I saw poor Miss Lemington-Smith lying dead on the ground.

I cannot help thinking that most of the household were rather glad when Bunty was dead. Anne Pargeter had done them a favour. Naturally, Celia was upset at first. They had been friends since school, I gather, but afterwards, once her body was taken away and we settled into that summer, I saw Mrs Sullivan change from a bundle of nerves into a calm and collected woman. She still had her silly moments, but they were always rather endearing. It would not do for her to become too sure of herself. I still have to make a living, after all.

I do wonder what Miss Lemington-Smith meant by telling Anne to ask Celia about why Percy was in a wheelchair. I've never asked – as a doctor I avoid getting into medical discussions with non-patients as they want a free diagnosis and I am not and never will be a part of this damned National Health Service they're talking about – but I'd always presumed the boy had polio.

Percy Sullivan

I've always been told that when I was about twelve months old, I managed to get out of my crib and get to the top of the stairs. That was when I couldn't work out what I was supposed to do, so I tumbled all the way to the bottom, breaking both my legs and damaging my spine. My legs healed but my spine didn't.

I don't remember much about it, but I sometimes have nightmares and in those nightmares someone gets me out of my crib and walks me to the top of the stairs, before pushing me down.

Was Bunty trying to say that Mummy pushed me down the stairs? She's silly and sometimes doesn't seem to know what to do with me and Lily, but I don't think she'd do something like that. I want to ask her, but I suppose I'm afraid of what the answer will be.

I really think it's better not to know bad things. Then I don't have to make up my mind about people. Like people have tried to force me to choose whether I think Anne is guilty or not. I don't want to have to decide if my mother did something unforgivable (inexcusable, reprehensible) to me when I was a baby.

Detective Inspector Andrew Marsh
Scotland Yard

The death of Miss Lemington-Smith would normally be left to the local police, but my stepbrother, Guy Marsh, asked me to look into it just in case it was related to that other business. I am grateful to young Percy Sullivan for giving me access to the testimonies he collected and it seems a good idea to add my own thoughts on the whole affair. I have also added another testimony from a certain Bert Little, which comes later in the narrative.

I can reveal now that Guy had gone to Lakeham Abbey at my behest. We had received a tip that there might be a smuggling ring in the area. It seemed an odd location, in the middle of the country, but it was also very secluded, far away from prying eyes.

Guy and I had grown up as brothers after my father married his mother. He took on the Marsh name to escape the scandal surrounding his father's death. It makes me laugh to think how much we hated each other when we first met. As only children – until the marriage – we both resented this other child who had come to steal half the attention. When it became clear that our parents could only concentrate on their love for each other, leaving us both out on a limb, we made a tenuous peace. When we served in the air force together during the war we became fire-forged friends and, by the time the war ended, true brothers in our hearts.

I knew that Guy was not settling into civilian life as easily as I had (and even I had moments when I was not sure what the hell it had all been for). His aid with the

Berlin Airlift helped a little, but we had seen things in Eastern Europe that easily turned a man to drink. I don't say that Guy was an alcoholic, but I do know that when I first asked him to look into the goings on at Lakeham Abbey, he was in a Chelsea pub staring into a glass of whisky. His breath suggested that it was not his first of the day and yet it was only just noon. If he had someone else to turn to, it might have helped. I did my best, but sometimes a man needs a woman's influence to help him heal. Our mother was at a loss, so I thought it might help him if I gave his life some purpose.

After the murder, I went along to Lakeham Abbey. Despite being related, I knew very little of the Sullivans. I found them to be a charming and quintessential English family. Professor Frederick Sullivan, who I gather was around forty-five years old, was your typical crumpled academic, with pipe and slippers, and one of those threadbare cardigans with leather elbow pads. Mrs Celia Sullivan, aged thirty-six, was a woman in her prime, utterly lovely, but also a bit scatty. I was not, however, convinced that she was as silly as she pretended. There was a little girl of two, but I didn't see much of her (she was hardly a suspect). And there was a teenage boy, in a wheelchair. Hotspur, I think Guy calls him, though his real name is Percy. He was a precocious young chap with a child's typical bloodlust where death was concerned. I got the feeling that if he ever got his legs working again, they'd never be able to catch up with him. As it was, he could still go either way in life. Saint or sinner; Sherlock Holmes or Moriarty on wheels. (I write this knowing that he is going to be reading it and think he will enjoy the joke!)

A Doctor Stanley Aitken, who I took to be somewhere in his late fifties or early sixties, was staying with them. He was again typical of his class. A bit pompous perhaps, but well-meaning and most solicitous of Mrs Sullivan, who was distressed by the death of her friend. I looked into him and found that he was one of those doctors who dealt mostly with middle to upper class women and their 'nerves'. I gather it left him quite rich, but also a bit lazy, so he had plenty of time to impose himself on upper class house parties, and was said to hardly ever go home to his Mayfair flat. I imagine this peripatetic lifestyle is how he finds his nervous patients.

Then there were the Carstairs. He – Angus Carstairs – was an arrogant sort; typical politician with a smooth, silky voice that hid a heart of solid rock. I could well imagine him sending a platoon of soldiers to their death without thinking twice on the matter. Mrs Carstairs was more poised and intelligent than Mrs Sullivan. Her looks were beginning to fade but she wore her expensive clothes well. There was the daughter too. Jennifer. She showed every sign of being a beauty like her mother, but was of an age where everything was too much trouble so she walked around with a sullen expression most of the time we were there. I got the impression that she was a bit put out at missing the excitement of a dead body.

The rest of the household were servants. I don't rule them out by any means, but many of them had worked at the Abbey for years, on and off. The only reason for concern is that none of them seemed to know exactly whom they were working for. They were hired through an agency, and most of the time they simply kept the downstairs rooms of the Abbey dust free whilst it was empty. There was a big thing about them not having access to the upper rooms.

Then there was the cook, Maudie, who had arrived with Miss Pargeter (of which more later). I didn't get much out of her. She was a taciturn sort who deferred to Anne Pargeter most of the time. Henry, young Percy Sullivan's attendant, was much the same. He had a stutter so it took a long time to interview him. However, he had been with the Sullivans for over ten years and his credentials appeared to be in order.

This brings us to Anne Pargeter. I might not have been as taken with her as Guy obviously was (and still is) but she was certainly an arresting young woman. She showed no particular sadness at Miss Lemington-Smith's death, apart from the usual polite regret one feels at the death of a stranger, but that is understandable as she hardly knew the woman. We know now that Miss Lemington-Smith found out the truth about Anne Pargeter, but the clues at the time did not point us in that direction.

Of the clues found on the scene, the cigarette butts on the roof were of the Camel variety. Half of Britain smokes those, and Mrs Sullivan (or maybe Anne Pargeter) kept a silver case full of them on the table in the drawing room for anyone to use, so that does not narrow it down.

There was something else, however, which we did not realise the importance of, but which threw everything into focus when the truth came out. When Miss Lemington-Smith's body was taken to the pathologist, a playbill for an old film was found in her pocket: *The Heart Knows.* I remembered it from my youth as a rather garish Regency potboiler. It was almost banned at the time, because of the low cut gowns worn by the actresses. Needless to say Guy and I snuck into the cinema to watch it and were disappointed to find that the film poster promised rather more than it delivered.

When we questioned Mrs Celia Sullivan about the playbill, she gave us what appeared at the time to be a satisfactory explanation. "Dear Bunty knew that it was the film playing on the night my husband asked me to marry him. She must have found an old playbill and planned to present it to us on our anniversary. It's funny. We were only talking about it at dinner recently and she did not let on."

At the time I took the explanation at face value, but soon everything I learned about Bunty Lemington-Smith suggested she was not capable of such generosity, especially where Mrs Sullivan's marriage was concerned.

59

We had problems gaining access to parts of the house. The owners had closed off the upstairs floors, and no one that we spoke to had keys. Or at least that's what they claimed. The Sullivans told me that they had been given the house at a peppercorn rent for the summer simply because not all the house was available.

In order for the police to gain access to the upper floors, they had to break down a door that went from the back kitchen to a flight of stairs presumably meant for servants in the past (I am told that the servants staying in the house – that is those who did not just come up from the town for the day – were sleeping on the second floor in the East wing).

It was clear that all the rooms were unused, though my colleagues in the local force tell me that there were so many little passageways and alcoves that they cannot be certain they found every room. That's the problem with these big old houses. Each owner adds some new wing or extension, and sometimes they completely block parts off, leaving spaces that are all walls and no doors. The only out of place thing that my colleagues noticed is that the corridors and staircases leading up to the roof had clearly been recently swept, albeit in a haphazard manner. A query to the servants brought back the response that none of them had done it, because they didn't have access. Somebody was obviously lying, but we had no proof or motive for Miss Lemington-Smith's death.

We found a smudged footprint which came from a woman's size five slipper. Of the household, Mrs Sullivan, Anne Pargeter and the teenager, Jennifer Carstairs, all wore that size. Miss Lemington-Smith wore a size seven, so it was definitely not her footprint.

When we finished our investigations at Lakeham Abbey, finding very little evidence in the process, we went to see Miss Lemington-Smith's Great Aunt, and it seemed that the mystery was solved.

Chapter Five

Detective Inspector Andrew Marsh Cont.

Miss Lemington-Smith's Great Aunt lived in Devon. As the Lakeham Abbey police resources were stretched, Guy and I agreed to go down and speak to her. Not that anyone else knew Guy was joining me. We kept that hush hush. It was quicker in his plane, and he was back at Lakeham Abbey by night so no one would miss him.

Great Aunt Jemima was a rather frightening woman, very Victorian in her manner and clothing. I don't think that the twentieth century had an effect upon her life at all, apart from a few sandbags still resting near the front door. She lived in a bungalow on the coast. It was overloaded with heavy oak furniture, framed family photographs, and seaside knick-knacks.

"I always knew this would happen," she said, pursing her dry old lips. "It's not the first time."

"That she's died?" I said, sure she could not really mean that.

"Well, of course it's the first time she's died." She gave me a well-deserved sneer. "It's not the first time she's tried it. She was a troubled child. Hard to love, some might say, although I am sure I did my best."

"You brought her up," Guy said.

"Yes. Her mother was a flighty one. Her father… Well, no one could even say who he was. It was all hushed up, of course, and her mother was married off to one of the servants. It didn't last long, and she drank herself to death when Bunty was a baby. The husband didn't want her, so I took her in. I always let her know of the sin of her birth. I don't believe in hiding these things."

Guy and I exchanged knowing glances. We had a 'Great Aunt Jemima' type somewhere in our lives, but we had been lucky enough not to have to live with her.

"She was born from wickedness and became wicked. I sent her away to boarding school, hoping they would beat some discipline into her. I thought that young Celia would help her, but she became obsessed with the girl, always wanting to be with her. I don't say she had romantic feelings for Celia. I don't think she was that way. But she was so cruel. Bunty could say things that cut you to the quick. Oh, the things she said to me, about how I thought I was a Christian but that I'd burn in hell. That I was a secret drinker. Heaven forbid." The old woman closed her eyes and I got the feeling that she would have quite liked a sherry. "As I was saying, Bunty tried to kill herself a few times. Celia never knew because we hid it from her. Like the time I had Bunty incarcerated, to try and get the devils out of her. We said she'd had an appendix operation that went wrong. Celia married whilst Bunty was still in the home and moved abroad quickly. I daresay she wanted to escape. Bunty tried to kill herself when she found out. So no, I'm not surprised she threw herself off the roof of that place. She's been meaning to do it for most of her life."

Anne Pargeter

Things certainly calmed down after Bunty Lemington-Smith's death, Hotspur. When the initial shock wore off, and it was decided that she had probably taken her own life, we all began to settle into summer. I had nightmares, but I don't think I was the only one. For me, Bunty's death was a repeat of what I had seen as a child. I could share that with no one but Maudie.

I heard the testimony that Doctor Aitken gave in court, about the conversation between Bunty and me. I cannot deny that it took place, just as he heard it.

You know now that Bunty was right about my mother,

and that I lied about who I really am. I want you to believe I did it for the best reasons, and that even if Bunty had told everyone the truth, it would not be an excuse for me to harm her.

One thing I want to assure you is that I don't believe that your mother would have ever willingly done anything to harm you. I have my own suspicions about what happened on the day you fell down the stairs, but I have nothing to back them up. I know your father shares these suspicions, so perhaps you should ask him.

Do you remember our picnic on the island, with Jennifer and Group Captain Marsh? And the wonderful surprise that was waiting there for you. It was about a week after Bunty's death, and the police were still coming and going. I know you wanted to be in the thick of things, but your mother was afraid of you becoming over-emotional. So I prepared a picnic for us. Remember those cherry tomatoes we put in a bag of salt? They are still the best I've ever tasted. Prison food is awful, but I suppose that's as it should be. We are considered the country's worst villains, so why should we have decent food when people in Britain are still under rationing?

At first, it was just going to be me, you, Jennifer and Henry, but Group Captain Marsh invited himself along (he seemed to have a habit of doing that). I can't say I complained. I liked him from the moment I saw him, when he landed his plane. It made me laugh to remember how he showed off, but when it came to the things he'd really done during in the war, he didn't like to talk about it at all. All he said, on that day, as we ate our sandwiches, was, "I flew a plane and a lot of people died, including good friends of mine and a lot of innocent Germans. They call me a hero, but believe me, it wasn't my finest moment."

"But the Germans bombed us too," you reminded him. "People died here."

"I know, Hotspur, and I don't really know how we could have done anything differently. I just don't see why I have to like it." I can still see his haunted eyes, and I understood then why the Berlin Airlift was so important to him. It was his way of helping the people he had bombed out of their homes.

Anyway, we took the boat over to the island, didn't we? Then Henry showed you his surprise. It was something I'd asked him to attempt, without knowing if it was possible.

He had built a tree house in the centre of the island, and it had a lift of sorts onto which you could roll your wheelchair and be winched up. He had worked on it with Guy over several days. You and Jennifer were enthralled and spent a good twenty minutes just trying out the lift. I think we all had a ride on it in the end!

Then, as we ate our picnic, Group Captain Marsh told us stories of the old owners of Lakeham Abbey. He was related to them in some way.

"The Marshes and the Lakehams have been connected for a long time," he told us, as we all bit into the cherry tomatoes, the juice rolling down our chins. "Not necessarily in a good way. One Miss Marsh married a Lakeham. They say she saw a ghost in this very house and it sent her insane."

"Like Anne's ghost," you said.

"Must be."

"But then she tried to murder her husband and blamed the ghost for it, so they had her incarcerated."

"Did she die in the asylum?" You really were ghoulish back then, Hotspur! Even Bunty's nasty death hadn't halted your love of the macabre.

"No, she was set free and married again," Guy explained. "But there was an incident on this very island. She used to meet her lover here, and one dark and stormy night..." He winked in my direction. "Lady Lakeham returned to seek her revenge on those who would wrong her – her husband, who had survived her attack, his mother, and her innocent cousin. That young woman drowned in the marshes in this very spot, her body sucked into the ground as her ladyship stood by and watched, laughing all the time. They say that the cousin haunted Lady Lakeham forever afterwards, cursing her children and any children born thereafter. It is her ghost that haunts this house to this day."

"Cor," you said. "Tell me more."

"Did she marry her lover?" Jennifer asked. "Or did he kill himself in anguish when he realised how mad she was?"

Guy laughed. "I don't know any more. It's all rubbish anyway. Just ghost stories. In real life, I'm sure that Lady Lakeham really was mad, but they covered it all up."

"Anne saw a ghost," you reminded him.

"Yes, I did," I admitted. "But I'm sure it's because I was very tired and thought that a dream was real."

"What if the ghost pushed Bunty off the roof?"

"Why would it, dear?" I was a bit concerned that you were taking it all so seriously, and began to wonder if Guy should be telling you such tales.

"Because Bunty went looking for it. The ghost, I mean. Bunty went where she wasn't supposed to go, so the ghost killed her to silence her."

"I don't think ghosts really harm the living, Hotspur," I said.

Afterwards, as Henry and Jennifer took you back to the tree house, I took Guy to task. "You shouldn't fill their heads with such things," I said. I wasn't really angry. It was hard to be angry with Guy. He was – is – incredibly handsome, but had such a hangdog expression sometimes, as if the whole world were against him. One could never say anything to deliberately hurt him. "They'll be having nightmares."

"Kids love this sort of thing," Guy insisted. "I know I did. Didn't you like ghost stories by the fireside, Anne? Then hiding under the bedclothes in case the bogeyman got you?"

"I didn't need a ghost for that," I said, feeling as

though he had shone a light into a part of my life that I did not want to share.

"Why?"

"Oh, you know, growing up in a children's home..." I've never been a very good liar and I don't think I convinced him then. I wanted to tell him the truth, but I had come to Lakeham Abbey for a reason. I know you think it was to take care of you and your family, and that is partly true.

I will admit to you now that when it came out in court that I had engineered being at Lakeham Abbey, it was correct. I had been looking for a way into the house. Not many in service like being in the country. They'd much rather be in the city, where there are pubs and cinemas. So my willingness to come here worked for me.

When I learned that your mother and father were taking the house for the summer, I went to one of my previous employers and told her I fancied working in this area (I said I had family here, which is not strictly untrue), and asked if she knew your mother and father. She didn't, but she knew Bunty Lemington-Smith, so she sang my praises to her. Given what I know about Bunty now, I'm surprised she bothered to mention me at all, but perhaps she liked the idea of having new scenery and people so she could continue her mental torture of poor Celia.

Anyway, back to our picnic on the lake. Group Captain Marsh and I had a few moments alone, whilst you, Jennifer and Henry messed around at the tree house. We chatted about nothing, but at the time it seemed as if it was the most important conversation ever. I was not yet in love with him, but I had a strong emotional response to him. Along with other emotions I cannot explain, as you are so young. I wanted to trust him with my secret, but I had spent too many years unable to trust anyone, and I was afraid of letting down my guard.

You, Jennifer and Henry returned, and you were full

of excitement. "Quickly, come with us," you insisted.

We followed you to the tree house which had a clear view up to the main house. "She was in that top window, I tell you she was." You were adamant.

"I saw her too," said Jennifer. "Really, she was in one of the windows."

"Who was, Hotspur?" Guy asked.

"The ghost. I saw her and so did Jennifer."

"Did you see anything, Henry?" Guy asked. Henry shook his head, and indicated that he had stayed on the ground.

"She was in a window on the fourth floor, looking this way," you said. "Honestly. She was dressed all in white. Then someone came and took her away. Isn't that right, Jennifer?"

"Yes, oh yes."

"Hotspur," I said, kneeling down to you, afraid that you were becoming over-excited. "Maybe it was one of the policemen looking around up there. Or maybe it was the way the light caught the window."

"No." You folded your arms across your chest. "No, it was her. I know it bloody was. We must go to the upper floors and investigate."

"We're not allowed up there," I reminded you. "It's not safe. Look at what happened to Bunty."

"You can do what you want," you said. "But I'm going to investigate."

"It's my fault," Guy said, when we had rowed back to the mainland and were walking up to the house. You, Jennifer and Henry had gone on ahead, because you were cross with us for dismissing your concerns. "I shouldn't have told him that story."

"I was the one who started with the ghost," I said. "So it's my fault really, when it probably was just a nightmare." I'll admit I was lying again. I had a feeling then that I knew who the ghost was, but she had disappeared from my room too quickly for me to prove it.

I've never been able to prove it, and because of that, people think I'm either mad or manipulative. Whatever they think of me, I am not a killer, Hotspur.

Percy Sullivan

We did see the ghost. We did! People think that because we're children, we're suggestible (impressionable, gullible), and that it was only the Group Captain's talk about ghosts and ladies sinking in the marshes that made us think we'd seen something at the window.

We'd been having a lovely day. Jennifer was being nicer to me, and Henry was teaching us things.

When he was pushing me around the island, we found some vole droppings at the water's edge, and Henry said that means there'll be a sizable habitat somewhere. We looked, but couldn't see any voles. We did see some squirrels running up a tree. And some mayflies. I think it's sad about the mayflies. They only live for a few hours, or one day at the most. Imagine having to fit everything into that time.

I feel like that now, with Anne's execution so near. I have so much to do, and I don't really know how I'm going to do it all. Henry said he would help. I think he liked her, because she was kind to him and made him Bakewell pudding for the picnic when she found out it was his favourite.

See, that's what Anne was like. She enjoyed making people happy, even if it was only something as simple as baking their favourite cake or finding their favourite brand of tea and making sure it was at the breakfast table.

When we were walking around the island, Henry seemed reluctant to go back. I asked why and he said it was because he thought Miss Pargeter and the Group Captain might want to be alone together for a while. I couldn't imagine why. At least not then.

Anyway, we decided to go back up in the tree house.

Jennifer went on ahead, and Henry winched me up on the lift. He stayed down on the ground at first. He said it was best in case there was a problem with the lift, but he was grinning as he said it and I wondered if he thought that Jennifer and I also wanted to be alone. I didn't think so, because to be honest I was a bit frightened (scared, alarmed) of her.

So for a while we sat saying nothing. Then Jennifer said, "Sorry I was a bit mean to you on the first day. Mummy said I was to take care of you, and I didn't want to because I thought it would be boring."

"I don't want you to take care of me," I said. "I hate it when girls come to play then treat me like some sort of pet. They soon get bored with that and forget about me."

"They're stupid," said Jennifer. "It's fun really, because you like the things I do, like dead bodies and ghosts. Mummy hates me talking about those things. It's not ladylike, she says. Do you read Agatha Christie?"

"Yes, all the time."

"Me too. We should put our heads together and see if we can solve Bunty's murder."

To be honest, I was afraid of her taking all the credit, but I agreed because she was a guest. And a bit frightening.

We spent the next ten minutes looking across at the house. We had a really good view from the tree. I pointed out to Jennifer where Bunty's body had been found (because Jennifer had been asleep and missed all the excitement), and then we tried to guess where the mad Lady Lakeham's cousin had drowned in the mud. It wasn't relevant to the case, but we agreed that it would improve our sleuthing skills to notice everything. I think we half expected to see a muddy hand sticking out of the marsh and were a bit disappointed when it didn't appear.

"I think I should cope quite well in an asylum," Jennifer said. "I should be placid and well-behaved until they knew I was not a mad woman and let me out."

"How do you know how you'd be?"

"Women are good at these things. It is our lot to suffer."

"But why get sent to an asylum in the first place?"

"Because I'll be a debutante and such things will happen to me in my life. They always do to debutantes in the films. Some evil man will try to marry me then have me locked away when I refuse. Then the love of my life will set me free. Unless I set myself free first."

"He'd be a bit upset if he turned up to rescue you and you'd already gone."

"I suppose so. In which case, I'll have to sit it out until he gets there."

Then I looked back towards the house and saw the figure in the window. "Jennifer, look!" I cried.

"What? What is it?"

"In the East wing on the fourth floor. There's someone there!"

"Yes! I see her," Jennifer cried. "It's a woman in white. Oh…she's gone now."

"Someone took her away," I said. "Did you see them?"

"I…I think so."

"We really have to get up there and investigate," I said. "Bunty fell from the roof, so there may be some clues."

"How are we going to get upstairs?" Jennifer asked. "Everything is locked."

"We'll have to break down a door."

"Percy," she said, sounding apologetic, "I don't mean to be rude, but even if we get through the door, you can't go upstairs, and I don't think I can lift you."

I cursed my useless spine. "Then I suppose I'll have to be lookout whilst you go." It spoiled things a bit and reminded me of all the things I could never do. It crossed my mind that kissing a girl might be one of those things, but goodness knows why that came to mind as there was no one I particularly wanted to kiss.

When we told Anne and the Group Captain, they

didn't believe us.

I didn't want to talk to them then, so I made Henry take me on ahead. Jennifer came with us.

Later, when we had tea in the nursery (Henry always goes off to do his own thing then – I think he's got a girlfriend in the kitchen), the Group Captain joined us. He let Lily sit on his lap, even though she dribbled all down his shirt. I think she really likes him, though, and he didn't seem to mind.

I worry about Lily sometimes. Mother is a bit scared of her, and Father does his best, but he's always working. So the only people who really show Lily any attention is me, Henry, and Anne when she was with us. I think Lily liked having the Group Captain as a new friend.

"We wanted to apologise to you, Hotspur," he said to me, as he fed Lily hot buttered toast. She wiped her sticky little fingers on his jacket, which only made him laugh. "And to you, Jennifer."

"Yes," Anne agreed. "We were very unfair not to take you seriously earlier. Of course, if you both say you saw something, then you must have seen it. Tell us more about it."

We told our story again, just as it happened.

"I'm not saying that you didn't see someone," Anne said. "But I do wonder if it might have been one of the servants. I've heard someone walking around up there, and I suspect that one of the servants who already worked here might have the key to upstairs."

"It didn't look like any of them," I said. "There was definitely a lady in white. But someone did take her away. A man."

"You didn't say it was a man earlier," the Group Captain said. "Was it a man, Jennifer?"

Jennifer looked at me, and then at them. Sometimes it's hard to be honest with grown-ups. Especially if they are convinced you're lying. "I'm not sure, but I saw something…"

"Of course you did, dear," said Anne. "Would you both like some more toast and jam?"

"No," I said, slamming my hand on the table. "I would like for people to stop thinking I'm bloody stupid because I'm in a wheelchair."

"No one thinks that, Hotspur," the Group Captain said. "We just wondered whether, because we were talking about ghosts earlier, that you saw something like a cloud reflected in the glass and immediately thought about the ghost."

"I know the difference between a cloud and a woman. And so does Jennifer."

But Jennifer was looking less certain.

"Yes, of course you do," Anne agreed. "It's all very intriguing, isn't it? What do you think is happening, Percy?"

"I think the ghost of mad Lady Lakeham has come back to haunt us, and is trying to frighten us from the house. That's why she killed Bunty." I admit now that it sounded very stupid. No wonder Jennifer rolled her eyes and sighed.

"Why do you think she's doing that?" asked the Group Captain.

"Because she's mad, of course."

"You don't think there might be another reason," Anne suggested. "I mean one that isn't supernatural."

"You said you believed us."

"I do believe you saw something, Hotspur, just as I did. But now I'm wondering if perhaps it was not a ghost at all, but a real person."

"Do you think that someone really did push Miss Lemington-Smith from the roof?" I asked.

"Oh, I don't know, dear." Anne looked unsure then. I think it's because I was a little boy and she didn't want me to think murders happened, but really I love all that sort of thing. It helped that I didn't much like Bunty, of course. If it had been Mother or Father, I might not have enjoyed it as much.

"We should go up there," I said. "What do you think, Group Captain?" I hoped that if Henry wouldn't take me, and Jennifer couldn't lift me, then they would.

The Group Captain did that thing of sucking in his breath. "I'm not sure, Hotspur. It could be dangerous."

"Excellent."

Doctor Stanley Aitken

Dreadful thing about Miss Lemington-Smith, dreadful. Of course, we all believed it was either an accident or suicide (if her Great Aunt was to be believed) at the time. No one could have guessed that the pretty Anne Pargeter had murder in her heart. She was always so charming. I saw through it, of course, and disliked her from the beginning. There was something about her that troubled me. Some people are just too nice. No one could be that perfect. It just isn't possible, though I know it will pain young Percy to hear that. I think he's got a bit of a crush on her.

Ah, well, we've all loved a wrong 'un at some point. Myself included. That's why I've never married. Once a devil woman gets hold of your heart, you can never escape.

Percy is young. He'll get over it. Not so sure about Group Captain Marsh, but he's the taciturn sort anyway. It was always certain that some woman would make him even more miserable than he already is.

He was a strange one that summer, inviting himself along, then going off on his own for hours.

At the time I wasn't sure of his motives. When I went into the local town one day to restock my tobacco, I saw him talking to someone outside the pub. A tall man, wearing a long Mackintosh. I must say he looked out of place in that hick town.

The Group Captain looked across and waved at me, then returned to his discussion. I went into the newsagents to get my tobacco.

"Hello, Doctor Aitken," the man behind the counter

said.

"I didn't realise you were known in these parts," said a voice behind me. It was the Group Captain. He'd followed me in.

"I come here from time to time," I said. "Friends in the area. I see that you have too."

"He's a friend," the Group Captain said. "He's staying in the area too."

I got the feeling there was more to it, because a few days later, I was in the town again and I saw the Group Captain following someone. At first I wondered if it was his pinstriped friend, but when I looked ahead I saw that it was Professor Sullivan's friends. What were their names? Oh yes. Sergei and Ivan. They had just dropped off some more pottery at the Abbey.

It was the day that a Mr Cohen joined us all for dinner at the Abbey, and a few weeks after Miss Lemington-Smith's death. I was under the impression that Mr Cohen was an associate of Sullivan's because they went upstairs for a while, to the professor's store room, and Mr Cohen came down with packages.

"It's pottery for the British Museum," Freddie Sullivan told us. "Mr Cohen is going to add it to the collection there."

"Wonderful," Celia said. "Perhaps Percy and I can come and see it when we visit Harley Street next week."

"I doubt it will be ready that quickly," said Mr Cohen. "I will tell your husband when it is available, Mrs Sullivan."

All the time, Group Captain Marsh was listening to this, with a thoughtful expression on his face. I don't know if he noticed, as I did, that Mr Cohen was rather emotional about the whole thing.

Percy Sullivan

The day before the trip to London, Jennifer and I had managed to get away from the adults and go exploring. I think her mother and father were still out looking for houses. My parents had gone into town for some reason. I can't remember what. Oh yes, something about Bunty's gravestone. Her Great Aunt wasn't willing to pay for anything too grand so Mummy had insisted we do something a bit better.

It was Anne's afternoon off so she and Group Captain Marsh had gone off somewhere in his plane, which was a bit much as he had promised to take me up in it. Maudie was looking after Lily.

I'm not sure where Doctor Aitken was. He came and went a lot, because of his patients.

So I gave Henry the afternoon off, telling him that I wanted to spend some time with Jennifer, which made him laugh. I'd not seen him laugh very often so it was rather a frightening experience.

First of all, I told him that I wanted to be on the second floor. "The old schoolroom is there," I said. "We're probably going to study." That also made him smile. "You can go about your business then, Henry."

"How are we going to work this out?" Jennifer asked when we were sure we were alone. "You can't get up the stairs."

"Yes, I'm aware of that. So I'll be a lookout, as you said. You'll have to do the exploring, then report back to me. Look in the bag on the back of my wheelchair, and you'll find a camera and some walkie talkies."

"Walkie whats?"

"Walkie talkies. An American uncle who was in the war gave them to me, though I'm not supposed to have them, really. They're brilliant. We can talk to each other, like on the telephone."

Jennifer did as I asked, then because she's a girl I had to show her several times how to use them.

"Mother loaned the camera to me for taking pictures of voles," I told her. "The film reel is brand new so take as many pictures as possible, then we can have them developed and analyse them together. We can keep in touch with the walkie talkies so you can tell me what you see."

"That's rather clever," she said. She put the camera strap around her neck, and held a walkie talkie in her hand, passing the other one to me.

"Yes, I rather thought so," I replied. "But first we have to find a way up there."

There were three doors leading to the upper floors. One at the end of each wing, that I think were used for servants, and one in the centre, above the grand hallway. Whereas the servants' doors were at the bottom of each staircase, the doors in the centre were at the top of the stairs. They were double doors, as high as the ceiling, but looked quite new compared to everything else in the house.

Jennifer climbed the staircase and tried to push the doors open, but to no avail.

"They're too heavy," she called back in a low voice.

"Never mind," I said. "We'll try the other two."

The door in the West wing would not open either. It looked as if the wood had swelled due to the damp.

"Last try and then we have to give up," said Jennifer. "We've no pictures at all yet, and no evidence of the ghost."

"We'll get it. You'll see."

The door in the East wing had not swelled in the frame, and I think it was the one the police used. I saw Jennifer reach for the handle, determined to give it a good tug. She suddenly lost her footing and fell into my lap. It wasn't the worst feeling in the world.

"Sorry," she said, jumping up after a few seconds. "It's already unlocked…" Sure enough, the door was ajar.

"Perhaps the police didn't secure it again," I said. "Gosh, we've been so stupid. We should have tried this one first."

"Are you going to sit here and keep watch?" asked Jennifer.

"Yes, I suppose I must." I was losing interest in the

scheme, because it only reminded me again of all the things I could not do. I did consider calling for Henry and asking him to help me up the stairs, but I had a horrible feeling he would be sensible and tell me that we shouldn't do it. "We should check the walkie talkies first. I put new batteries in this morning." I pressed the button. "Are you there, Jennifer? Over."

"Of course I'm here," she said, giggling. "I'm standing right next to you."

"If you're not going to take this seriously…"

"Oh, I am. Of course I am." She pressed the button on her walkie talkie. "Testing, one, two, three. Over and out."

"I suppose we won't really know if they work until we're apart," I said. "So. Are you going up there or not?"

"Yes, just give me a minute." She adjusted the camera around her neck, and clipped the walkie talkie onto the waist of her skirt. I think she was a bit afraid of going upstairs alone, because she did that thing of swallowing hard before she took the first step.

"Be careful," I said, suddenly afraid myself. What if the ghost pushed Jennifer off the roof? I'd be responsible because I'd let her go up there alone. "Jennifer," I said into the walkie talkie, when she was only half way up the stairs.

"Give me a chance," she hissed back down the stairs.

"I just wanted to say don't go up to the roof, that's all. It's not safe. Over."

"Oh, I'll be alright. I shan't go near to the edge."

"Jennifer," I said a few minutes later.

"What now? Over."

"I just wondered where you were. You'd gone quiet. Over."

"Because there's nothing to tell yet. There's just a long corridor with lots of doors going off them. Most of them are locked. Over."

"Roger that."

"Roger who?"

"It's what you say when you agree with something or understand. Over."

"Oh. Roger that then."

It seemed to take an age before she spoke again.

"Percy. Over."

"What? Over."

"I've found some cigarette butts near to the next flight of stairs. Shall I take a picture? Over."

"Yes, do. Over."

"They're Camels again, over."

The police hadn't mentioned cigarette butts inside the house, only on the roof. I wondered if someone had been up there since.

Things went quiet again. I can't tell you how nervous I was for Jennifer. I could hear her footsteps above me, as she moved along the corridor.

"I'm taking more pictures. Over."

"What of? Over."

"Lots of things. Just in case. Over."

I heard footsteps right above me again. "Jennifer. Are you coming back? Over."

"No. I'm going up the next staircase. The one in the middle of the house. It isn't blocked off on this side and I want to see what's up there. Over."

"Jennifer. There's someone right above me. Over." I paused to listen. "It's coming this way. No, it's stopped and it's going back the other way. Jennifer, it's coming towards you. Over." Several minutes passed in which all I could do was sit and wait.

"Jennifer? Over."

"Shush. Someone's coming and I'm hiding! Over!"

Hiding from whom? Or what? I wished I'd never sent her up there. I wished she would come back. I wished I could climb the stairs and help her. As I thought about it, I was determined to do it. I wheeled closer to the staircase, and caught hold of the bannister, pulling myself up. My back screamed back in agony, but I was determined to go and help her. I could perhaps get the ghost's attention and make it leave her alone.

As soon as I stood up, I immediately fell onto the step, causing more pain. But I ignored it, and started to try and pull myself up each step. I managed three steps then had to stop. I no longer had the walkie talkie, because I couldn't hold onto it and get up the stairs. "I'm coming, Jennifer," I said, hoping she was close enough to hear me.

The effort was too much for me. I started to sweat and then I started to feel faint. Great. I had a girl as a friend and now I was going to show myself up by fainting in front of her. Or what if I fainted and left her alone to be murdered by the ghost?

Suddenly everything went black.

I woke up on my bed. Jennifer was sitting on the edge, and Henry stood at the end, looking very angry with me. He doesn't talk much or very often, but he told me how stupid I had been and that I was lucky he wouldn't tell my mother. "The upstairs r-rooms are out of b-bounds," he said. "And for g-good reason. Don't g-go up there again."

He left me and Jennifer alone.

"What did you see?" I asked her, pulling myself up to sitting position, and feeling much happier knowing that she was safe.

"I don't know," she said. "I was so scared I closed my eyes. Then when whoever it was walked past where I was hiding, I ran back down as quickly as I could. I'm sorry, Percy but I lost the camera and the walkie talkie. They're both still up there."

"How could you be so stupid?" I fell back on the bed.

"Hey, I was the one risking my life upstairs whilst you were all safe and nice in your wheelchair, so don't have a go at me!"

She flounced from the room and I felt a bit bad, but I didn't want to tell her that.

The next morning, when I woke up, I found the camera and walkie talkies on my bedside table.

That was the day Mother took me to London to Harley Street. I wanted the doctor to tell me that I would walk again, but he only made the same promises that all other doctors made. I'm never going to walk.

That night, at the hotel, Mother got all sentimental and started to sing 'You'll Never Know'. I quite liked it at first, because Mother is never like that with me. Then for some reason it made me think of Jennifer, so I told my mother to shut up and let me go to sleep.

Chapter Six

Celia Sullivan

I do recall a Mr Cohen coming for dinner. I'm not quite sure what that has to do with Anne and what happened next. I am certain she never met him before that day.

It had been a sad time for us, with dear Bunty's death. Yet things had become more relaxed. We seemed to laugh more, and I didn't have that tight feeling in the pit of my stomach that came from wondering if she was going to insult Emma and Angus. Or my mothering skills.

Poor Bunty. We met at boarding school. I was only six at the time, and very timid. My father died when Percy was a baby. I loved him, as one should love one's papa, but he was a very strict and exacting man. Everything in the house had to be just so, and if not, then my mama and I would be in trouble. He never raised his hand to us, or even his voice, but we knew when he was angry. Anything might upset him, even a doll left on the sofa. I always had to remember to put my toys away. Once, one of my nannies took the blame, but he dismissed her. After that, Mama warned nannies not to say they'd done anything they hadn't, no matter the consequences for us.

I think that was why Mama decided to send me away to boarding school. So that I wouldn't irritate Papa so much. I know I was prone to do it all the time.

I was a nervous little thing and had hardly any friends. Then I met Bunty. She had no one at all. Just an elderly and rather terrible great aunt who lived in Devon. Great Aunt Jemima would send Bunty long letters, detailing her niece's failings. Bunty was more used to life than I was, so she helped me by telling me whenever I did anything wrong. Sometimes I'd be upset with her, because I was sure I'd done nothing, but she would remind me that she was only trying to help me be better for Papa. I honestly believed that all she ever wanted was to save me from trouble.

I once took her home with me for the holidays and my father did not like her at all. She, on the other hand, really approved of him, and spent all the time trying to please him. I was rather put out, because I felt I had lost an ally, but Bunty assured me she was only pretending to like him for my sake. I'm not so sure about that. Once I overheard him say to her, "I know exactly what type of person you are, so don't try your tricks on me." I don't know what brought that about and when I asked Bunty she denied it ever happened.

She was my friend for over thirty years and it was so odd not having her here. There was no one to guide me anymore. When I ask Freddie for guidance, he says, "Celia, I don't want to change anything about you." Which is no help at all, really.

It meant I had to start thinking for myself. That was difficult at first, but as the weeks passed, and Bunty's death was nothing more than a sad memory, I began to feel differently. Anne was particularly good with me, which makes me feel ashamed now of how rude I had been to her over dinner the night before Bunty died.

Yes, Anne is a pretty girl, but Freddie has never given me a reason to doubt him. In fact, I don't think he looks at her very much at all, except to say thank you for his cup of tea.

"I'm sorry, Anne," I said to her one day. I think it was the morning Percy and I went to London to Harley Street. I had thought of taking Jennifer as company for him, but she and Percy seemed to have had a falling out.

"Sorry, Mrs Sullivan? What on earth for?"

"The other week, after dinner, I was very rude to you."

"You were under a lot of strain," she said, so kindly that I do sometimes wonder how such a pleasant girl could kill someone.

"Oh, I don't think so," I said, but as her words sunk in, I realised that I had been under a lot of strain. Not just that night, but for a long time. In the weeks following Bunty's death, I somehow felt less clumsy and awkward. I even held Lily more, because I had been so afraid after…

That's a story for another time.

Freddie had been willing to go up to Harley Street with Percy, but at the last minute a Mr Rubenstein said he was coming to dinner and Freddie could not put him off. Mr Rubenstein was collecting more pottery for another museum. Soon, Freddie's pieces will be in every museum in the world!

So Percy and I got on the train to London. Henry came along too, but when we reached Paddington, I told him to go off and do something on his own. I had never really pushed Percy's wheelchair and I was afraid of getting it wrong, but I think I managed rather well. Admittedly, I did push him through that puddle and we got a bit wet, but we both thought it was rather funny.

The specialist on Harley Street, Mr Sethwick-Green, was very pleased with his progress. He is certain Percy will walk again one day. But every new doctor says that, to show that they intend to do things better than the last. Sadly, they never quite manage it.

Then, because Sethwick-Green was new to us, he asked me how Percy came to be in the wheelchair.

"He climbed out of his crib and got to the top of the stairs," I said. "He's really rather clever about such things."

"Was the side of the crib not up? Or the bedroom door shut?" Mr Green asked. I felt a little uncomfortable then, as if he doubted me.

"Well, yes, I'm sure both of those things were in place. You see, it was Nanny's day off, and I was very tired, so my friend, Bunty, told me to take a nap whilst he was sleeping. 'That's what it says in the books, Celia', she told me. 'You should sleep when they do. I'll sit downstairs and listen out for Percy'. So I did that, very grateful to Bunty for her help, but I am certain I did put up the side of his crib and shut the door…"

Then Percy said, "Why are you crying, Mother?" I hadn't realised I was, which was very silly of me. But I was crying, because he was my darling baby boy and I would never have let anything happen to him. And if that was the case, then there was only one way he could have climbed out of his crib. Suddenly I saw it, as clear as if I had been standing there, watching it take place. I understood then why I had been so afraid to hold Lily, because I had been told that what happened was my fault. In many ways it was my fault. I should have known better, but it is strange how one allows something poisonous to fester for fear of speaking the truth.

Of course, I said nothing of this to the doctor. "I see, Mrs Sullivan," he said. "I see." And I could see my failure as a mother in his eyes, and I wanted to scream at the injustice of it all, because I would never be able to prove the truth.

We left then, and I was so happy, but also sad. I was happy that I knew I would never hurt Percy or Lily, but I was sad because I had spent so many years holding my children at arm's length, afraid that I would fail them as a mother. Was it possible to put things right? Lily was young and might not realise how much I had neglected to show my love, but Percy had ten years of me keeping my distance. How could I put that right? What if they rejected me?

We went to tea at The Ritz, and had the most delicious sandwiches. I was giddy with happiness, and I suspect the *maitre d'* thought I was drunk. Then, just before we had to get the train back, we went to the British Museum. I hadn't thought of the steps, but some kind men helped me to carry Percy's wheelchair.

We had a good look around, and Percy told me everything about the artefacts. He is every bit as clever as his father is and is going to be a great man someday. I told him so, as part of my newfound resolution to let him know how precious he is to me.

When I saw one of the custodians, I asked him for Mr Cohen. I thought we might offer the dear man tea at the station before we left.

"Mr Cohen, madam?" The man looked confused.

"Yes, Mr Cohen. He's an associate of my husband's and he brought some Etruscan pottery here last week ready for showing. I know the pottery won't be on show yet, but it would be nice to say hello to Mr Cohen."

"There's no one of that name here, madam," the man said. "Are you sure it's the correct name?"

"Oh, perhaps not," I said, feeling silly again. "My husband has so many friends coming and going. Or perhaps we just have the wrong museum." It was very likely I'd got it wrong. When we got back home, Freddie as much as told us so.

That night I tucked Percy into bed, and for the first time in a long time I sang to him; "*You'll Never Know.*"

After a few minutes he said, "Please be quiet and let me go to sleep, Mother." But I think that he secretly enjoyed it.

Anne Pargeter

On the day you went to Harley Street. Guy and I went flying. It started out so well, before going horribly wrong as the past insisted on catching up with us both.

He popped into the kitchen in the morning, just to invite me. "I'm told it's your afternoon off and I've got some deliveries to make up north. How do you fancy a trip in the Lancaster? We'll fly up to Flamborough Head and have tea at Robin Hood Bay. We'll be back by dinner. What do you say?"

"I say 'Yes, please'."

I'd never been in an aeroplane. I can't explain how

exhilarating it was, flying above the clouds, looking down at the patchwork of fields below us and the tiny cars, like toys on a tiny racetrack. I had thought I would be terrified, but I wasn't. I loved every second of it, and wished the flight could go on forever. I still dream of that day. I imagine escaping the prison and flying off into the great blue yonder. But in the dream I'm not in a plane. I'm actually flying, with my arms outstretched. Then I feel a strong hand take mine and I look and see that it's Guy, flying with me…

He flew (in the plane!) in to Flamborough via the North Sea, and the cliffs rose before us, as the plane flew higher and higher.

"This is where the Dambusters practised," he told me. "Here and at Lady Derwent Reservoir in Derbyshire."

"You share a name with one of them," I said.

"Would it disappoint you to know that my real name is George?"

"Really?"

"Yes."

"So why Guy?"

"It's a nickname that my stepbrother, Andrew, gave to me when we were kids. He was very much into American gangster movies at the time. James Cagney and all those. You know? So when we first met, he said, 'I don't like you, guy, so keep out of my way'. Our parents – his father and my mother – thought it was hilarious, so the name stuck. I was livid at the time, because I thought they were all laughing at me. But I've come to like it over the years. So when I decided to reinvent myself, at the age of sixteen, I took that as my Christian name and took on my stepfather's surname."

I wanted to ask him why, but I was afraid it might lead to me telling him how I too had reinvented myself. "I like it," I said. "It suits you better than George."

After we landed, we made the delivery – some stationery for a local company. Guy said, "It's not exactly what I expected to be doing after the war, but it pays to keep the Lancaster in the air."

Then we went along to Robin Hood Bay and walked down the hill to the beach.

I must admit I was more than capable of being silly about fashion, particularly if I was with a man I really liked, but on that day common sense had taken over and I had worn sensible shoes. The descent was still treacherous, and occasionally I had to grab Guy's arm. I daresay that now he thinks I was being deliberately coquettish. Perhaps I was, but I meant it in the same innocent way that all girls do when they're with an attractive man. I am not the siren he believes I am. Before him I had seldom gone out with other men, and those relationships I had were rather chaste and formal. I daresay this is because I was afraid of giving too much of myself.

"What did you want to do when you left the Air Force?" I asked him as we sat on the sea wall.

"I'm not sure. Before the war I worked in Whitehall as a parliamentary secretary. I had thought I'd go into politics myself, but now I'm not sure."

"Really? So do you know Mr Carstairs at all?"

"Oh yes, I know Angus."

"That sounds ominous."

"He's not as bad as some. But they all have their secrets. There's something that happens to a man when he gets power. He begins to think he's untouchable. When the war ended, I found I lost respect for most of the politicians. They had promised us a brave new world, free of Hitler, yet many of my friends came back to find they had nothing left. Even now, some three years after the end of the war, we're still rationed. Yet you can bet the boys at Westminster aren't. That's when I decided I didn't want to be a politician. I don't want to send young men to war, whilst I sit comfortable in a Westminster bar, free from the restrictions the rest of the country has to face."

"So what now?"

"I think I'd rather like to set up my own airline. International travel is really going to take off soon – excuse the pun – with even lower income families able to go abroad and I'd like to be a part of that. So I'm saving as much as I can, until I can afford a small passenger plane."

"How exciting!"

"Yes, I think so." He paused for a moment as if he was deciding whether to tell me something. "I could start straight away, but it means making a big decision on whether to give up my principles."

"In what way?"

Guy breathed in deeply. "Tell me about yourself now. I know so little of you. Other than that you're a consummate professional and the best housekeeper the world has ever known."

"Thank you." I bowed my head graciously. "I'm afraid that's probably all there is to know."

"Whatever made a girl like you decide to become a dogsbody for rich families?"

"I don't consider myself a dogsbody." I laughed. "I'm much better at delegating than you might think."

He turned to me and took me gently by the shoulders. Our eyes met. "You always deflect questions with a joke. I wonder why, Anne."

"What there is to know about me is very boring." That was not quite true, but I had built too high a wall around myself to let it fall, even if the means of its destruction came in the guise of very arresting steel-grey eyes. I moved away slightly, unnerved by his touch. He seemed to realise and let me go.

"I doubt that. Let's start with your childhood. Where were you born?"

"Derbyshire." It was not a lie. Millions of people have been born in Derbyshire, so it would hardly narrow things down.

"Where in Derbyshire?"

"A little town called Matlock." I braced myself,

because that was getting a little bit too close. But thousands of people were born there, and he could hardly know that my mother was just passing through when she went into labour.

"And your parents died when you were little. Is that correct?"

"Yes." My first and biggest lie since the question and answer session began. "Maudie brought me up and I went into service with her when I was old enough." That was only half a lie. I had been old enough when it all took place and went into service almost immediately.

It is startling how upper class people would not dream of putting their own twelve-year old children to work, but are quite happy for a mere child to spend eighteen hours a day making sure their homes were warm and clean and their food was on the table on time. "I must have done every job in every house in which we worked." That was the truth, so I felt happier about it. "Then when I was twenty I decided that I would become indispensable to my clients."

"Your clients?" He raised an eyebrow and grinned.

"Yes, my clients. Since the Great War, upper class families have lost most of their servants. No one in their right mind wants to work an eighteen hour day cleaning up after others when they can work for ten hours in a factory or office, with two days off a week, for twice the pay. Many upper class women find they have to do a lot of the jobs the servants used to do, including organising them. To be perfectly frank, most of those ladies don't have a clue how to run a house, because it was always done for them. So I decided to create a bespoke service that took care of all their needs, and even the needs they didn't realise they had. If they need a housekeeper, I'll be a housekeeper. If they need a nanny, I'll do that too. If they need a cook, I'm perfectly capable of preparing a meal every bit as delicious as Maudie's. I was determined to charge well for the service too. After all," I said, "I'm going to be worn out by the time I'm forty so I might as well have a good pension on which to retire."

"And what are you going to do when you retire?"

"I'm going to buy a house by the sea. Perhaps even in this very bay. Then I'm going to write terrible potboiler books and keep a dozen cats."

"I approve," he said. "Yet none of this tells me where you were before you began your quest for domestic domination."

"I told you. I was in service."

"So why do I feel you're leaving an awful lot out? You're too intelligent to have been in service, Anne. My mother had a lot of maids over the years and they were generally a dull and rather stupid lot."

"No wonder your mother had a lot of maids if that's how you all considered them," I murmured.

"I'm sorry," he said. "I must have sounded like a dreadful snob."

"Yes, you did." I stood up. "Come on. I'm ready for a cup of tea. There's a café halfway up the hill."

"Anne…" He took my hand and drew me back to him. "I really am sorry for what I said. But there's no denying that you're a cut above the rest." He looked at me and I thought my heart would melt. "If I'm honest, you're a cut above everyone. Celia Sullivan, Emma Carstairs. Neither of them hold a candle to you. You have this light shining within you, and it draws us all, like very willing moths to a flame. This is why I'm convinced that your story is not as prosaic as you pretend."

"You think that someone who is lowly born can't be special?" I bristled slightly. My mother had come from nothing, yet she too had an inner light that drew others to her.

He scoffed slightly. "I'm always going to say the wrong thing to you, aren't I? I'm convinced that you can be anything you want to be. I'm just not convinced it happened the way you say it did. But it's your life and as

I have my own secrets, I respect your right to keep yours."

As his head drew nearer to mine, I wanted him to kiss me. But we were talking about my secrets and I was afraid that if he did kiss me, it would cause those secrets to tumble from my lips into his mind. I wondered too about his secrets. There was too much between us for us to take our relationship beyond friendship. Now I know there was even more between us than I imagined, and I wonder at the chain of events that brought us together that summer.

I pulled away and we walked up the hill together in silence. My inability to be honest had created an impasse. Luckily, the hill was so steep we were too out of breath to really talk. We went into the café and took our seats, ordering tea and a slice of bread pudding each.

"I realise," he said, after we had said nothing to each other for about fifteen minutes, "that it's very unfair to press you when I am not even willing to talk about my early life."

"Why don't you like talking about it? Was it that painful?"

He looked at me levelly. "Let's do a quid pro quo. I'll tell you something if you tell me something."

"I'm not sure… I…"

"I'm happy to go first."

"Very well. I reserve the right to silence…" I almost added 'on the grounds it might incriminate me', but that was rather too close for comfort, "…if I don't want to answer."

"Tough terms, but I'll agree to it. I was born in Esher, Surrey."

"I've already told you I was born in Matlock, Derbyshire."

"That's a spa town, isn't it?"

"I believe so."

"You believe?"

"I was very young when I left there." Only a week

old, as it happened. I didn't tell him that.

"My father was something of a reprobate," Guy said.

"Yes, so was mine…"

"Oh dear. I hope we're not going to turn out to be brother and sister. That would upset all my plans."

That made me laugh, and it helped to lighten the mood a little. "As far as I'm aware, I'm an only child."

"So was I. Until my mother remarried and I gained a stepbrother."

"Andrew, the policeman?"

"Yes, Andrew the policeman."

"He seems nice."

"He wasn't always that way. Then again, neither was I. We clashed a bit as children. Both wanting all the attention, having been only children. We got over it."

"Did your mother and father divorce?"

"No, it's your turn," he said, giving me a lopsided grin.

"I don't have a stepbrother called Andrew." The mood was becoming more playful.

"That's cheating!"

"I don't have any step-siblings."

"Your mother didn't remarry?"

"She didn't even divorce."

"Ah. So your parents stayed together until they died?"

"Something like that." The truth was far too complicated to tell, and it would give too much away. "It's your turn now."

"Is it?" he asked. "I've lost track a bit."

"Did your parents divorce?" I asked again.

"No, not quite. My father died."

"I'm sorry."

"It's your turn."

"I…I didn't know my father." It was the truth and I thought it might explain my reticence, even though it was not quite the whole story.

"I see…"

"You disapprove?" I raised an eyebrow. I knew I was

testing him and that I was being a little bit unfair about it.

"Anne, no. Not at all." He looked very handsome when he was flustered. That natural diffidence of his came to the fore and he seemed more like a little boy than a war hero. "Is that why you were afraid to tell me? Because you thought I'd disapprove of you being born out of wedlock?"

"I wasn't." I smiled at catching him out. "Not really. It's complicated. My mother married young then regretted it. That's all I can say." So far I hoped I had said nothing that could link me to past events.

"Fair enough."

"Your turn again, George," I teased.

"Don't call me that," he said, his grey eyes darkening. "That was my father's name and I would rather not use it."

Even then I didn't see the connection. There were a lot of men called George in England, on account of it being the name of two kings within living memory. "I'm sorry, Guy." The air became tense again. Strange how he could make a *faux pas* and I forgave it, but if I did it, he sulked.

We sat at the window, looking out as hikers and holidaymakers walked up and down the hill, but we did not speak for what seemed a long time.

"It's alright," he said, finally. "It's not your fault. You're not supposed to know what that name means to me."

"What does it mean?" I asked, softly.

"It means a man who shamed my mother at every opportunity, chasing around after showgirls and actresses. I probably do have brothers and sisters out there. My father was anything but discreet… What do you think killed Bunty Lemington-Smith?"

The question came from nowhere, and I was only just analysing what he had said about his father – a man named George – chasing showgirls and actresses. It really was rather too close for comfort.

"I'm not sure what you mean. Don't you mean who killed her? She killed herself, didn't she?"

"No, I don't think so, Anne. Don't you feel it when you're in that house? That it's a living, breathing creature?"

"Sometimes," I whispered.

"The house killed her, Anne. I'm sure of it. Because there's evil at the heart of the Abbey."

"What makes you say that, Guy?" My heart pounded in my chest. I knew what he was going to reply before he said it.

"My father died in that house. Killed by one of his actress floozies. Or her daughter. It's all a bit woolly. But I have no doubt that it was the house that really killed him. It brings out the worst in people."

The room began to swim before my eyes, and I could taste the spices from the bread pudding in the back of my throat. "I need… I have to…" I got up from the table and lumbered outside where I was sick on the pavement.

"Anne," he said, his voice coming from a long way away. He put his hand on my shoulder and I had to resist the urge to push him away. "Anne, I'm sorry. I didn't mean to distress you. It's all rather ghoulish, I admit. Are you alright?"

I tried to nod, but it made me feel dizzier than ever. All I could think, as he led me back up the hill, was Guy's father was George Peterson and that my mother and I had both been at Lakeham Abbey on the night he died…

Detective Inspector Andrew Marsh

Of course I know about the George Peterson case. It was how my father, who was the Commissioner of Scotland Yard at the time, met my stepmother, Vera. She brought her son, Guy, who was fourteen at the time, into our lives. She was Peterson's widow, but I believe she and George had been estranged for some time, due to his being something of a stage door Johnny. In fact, my stepmother had been an actress when they first met.

The facts, as we know them, are as such: Some time before the war began, George Peterson had been seeing the actress, Eleanor Grace. The affair lasted quite a bit longer than his usual relationships and was said by the gossip columns to be serious, perhaps leading to marriage. The stumbling block was Peterson's marriage to my stepmother, Vera, which had not yet legally ended. Eleanor Grace had a daughter, twelve-year old Mary-Ann Lakeham; the product of an early and unfortunate marriage to a man who went mad and ended up in an asylum. Such stories were not unheard of in the Lakehams. The family has had a long and troubled past.

The rest of what we know can only be surmised. During a weekend at Lakeham Abbey, George Peterson fell from the roof and died of horrendous injuries. One might have put it down to an accident, but Eleanor Grace went missing and her clothes were found on a beach near Filey. The daughter, Mary-Ann, disappeared completely, and nothing was heard of her from that date. A few days after Peterson's death, the police received a letter from Eleanor Grace admitting to the murder of George Peterson, but tests on the handwriting suggested it might have been a forgery. Neither Eleanor Grace nor her daughter were ever seen again from that date.

As can be imagined, the case was something of a cause celebre; a beautiful actress, about to make her mark in Hollywood, her dead lover, and a missing girl. No one knew what had happened, nevertheless, the newspapers had a marvellous time coming up with all sorts of theories. Then the war happened, and it fell out of public consciousness and, perhaps understandably, to the back of the police files. When he was sixteen, my stepbrother changed his name from George Peterson to Guy Marsh, because any mention of the familiar name would lead to others asking 'Any relation to…?' and he did not like to talk about it.

It was not even the reason my stepbrother went to Lakeham Abbey, though understandably the case was on our minds when I asked him to go there, and again when Bunty Lemington-Smith died in very similar circumstances to George Peterson. Guy had not much love for his father, because of the pain caused to Vera, but I suspect the anguish of his father's death lay deep down. I often wonder if Guy had hoped that one day his father would return.

So, yes, whilst others had forgotten the case, in our family it was still remembered. Imagine my surprise, when at the end of August, whilst my stepbrother was still carrying out investigations at the Abbey, I received an anonymous note saying that Mary-Ann Lakeham had returned to the Abbey and was going by the name of Anne Pargeter.

Chapter Seven

Celia Sullivan

The day began well enough. We decided to hold a garden party at the end of the season, and had invited some locals to share in our entertainment. We thought it would make a nice change for everyone after the austerity of the war. There were cake stalls and tombolas and carnival rides, and a gypsy fortune teller (who was really Anne, made up and wearing lots of silk scarves). The children were very excited. I sat on the carousel with Lily in front of me. I don't think I'd ever dared to do something like that, especially since Percy's accident, but she adored it, shouting, 'More, Mama, more, Mama' every time it stopped.

I felt more relaxed than I had for a long time and began to believe that I could be a good mother. It's ironic to think, now that the truth has come out, that I have Anne Pargeter to thank for my newfound confidence with my children. She had cut a malignant tumour from our lives and she had gently guided me into spending more time in my children's company. I even began to wonder if Freddie and I could have another baby. I'm still young enough. Of course, it would mean moving to a bigger flat or even a house, but I would not mind that.

It was time to face my life head on now that I no longer had the shadow of Bunty hanging over me. Still, somewhere, in the back of my mind, I heard her nasal voice saying, 'You can barely cope with two children, Celia'. So I decided to enjoy the moment and worry about the future when it happened.

I must confess I enjoyed playing lady of the manor,

judging the cakes stalls, and handing out prizes to children who ran the egg and spoon race. I could not help but notice my son, sitting on the sidelines, unable to join in. Anne had even allowed for that, and whatever else she has done, I bless her for the kind thought. Before going off to be *Madame Fortuna*, or whatever it was she called herself on that day, she produced half a dozen wheelchairs. I learned later that she had procured them from the local cottage hospital.

"Now," she said, "a very special race, and not one for the fainthearted. Percy, come and take your place. You too, Jennifer. And I need five more contenders."

Percy and Jennifer seemed to have got over whatever fall out they had the day before I took him to Harley Street, but they still had not spent a lot of time together over the previous weeks. Several times, Jennifer had chosen to go out with her parents, looking for their new house. I had tried to find out from Percy what had happened between them but he was rather reticent about it all. They were civil with each other, but they were not as close as I'd hoped they'd become.

I do worry about Percy. Freddie and I can't live forever, and I fear my son will end up alone. We've made sure he will always have a nurse, even if it is not Henry, but that's not the same as having someone in your life that you love. Oh, don't think I expected Jennifer to sign up to be his carer for the rest of his life. The girl was still only a child. I just thought that if he had one girlfriend, it would not seem so difficult for him to get another.

As the sun blazed down on us a few more children went to join in the race, but there seemed to be some reluctance to fill the last wheelchair.

"I suppose I'd better do it," said Guy. He had been standing watching Anne in that admiring way we could not fail to notice. I knew they had spent some time together and I was glad of it. He looked much happier than when he first arrived at Lakeham Abbey. And come to think of it, so did she.

He sat in the remaining wheelchair, looking incongruously large next to the children. This made everyone laugh. Anne went over to him and whispered something to him that made him grin.

"Are we ready?" cried Anne. She raised a starting pistol and after a count of three, fired.

The race was just the funniest, and most wonderful, thing I had ever seen. Everyone but Percy floundered, unable to control their chairs. My son, with years of practice, and upper arms prepared to deal with a wheelchair on grass, began to move forward at a steady pace, whilst everyone else brought up divots in the grass with their wheels, or somehow managed to turn their chair in entirely the wrong direction. What I remember most was the determination on Percy's wonderful little face. I had seen that so many times in his life, but never had it been mixed with so much joy. My lad made it easily past the finishing line, and I was more than proud to present him with his prize – a small gold-plated cup. It had only cost a few shillings, but to us it was priceless and still sits on our mantelpiece.

"Well done, Percy," said Jennifer, still laughing at her own efforts. She came in second. Eventually.

"Thanks." His face was already red from exertion but I do believe he also blushed a little.

"You're really good at this."

"You did okay too. Better than the others. I think Group Captain Marsh is still on the first line." I looked towards Guy who was laughing and still applauding Percy, along with everyone else.

"Shall we go and get some orange squash, Percy?"

"Yes, alright. Can you push me though? My arms are killing me."

"Yes, of course."

Off they went, chatting and laughing together. Despite it being what I wanted, I prayed, 'Please let him be my little boy for a while longer'. I had already wasted so much time worrying about doing wrong by him.

A little while later, I went to see *Madame Fortuna,* and paid a shiny silver sixpence to have my fortune read. Even though I knew it was Anne, I was impressed by her ability to take on the character. She had put *Ambre Solaire* on her face and arms, and covered her lower face with a veil. Her eyes were heavily kohl'd, giving her a very mystical look indeed.

Inside the tent was a small table, with a crystal ball in the centre, though I think that in reality it was a snow globe, as I could see a Father Christmas figure and a red-nosed reindeer inside it. Incense burned in a jar and, with the decorations, the tent could have been somewhere in the desert; the home of a Bedouin. It made me think of Rudolph Valentino in *The Sheik*.

"Madame Fortuna sees all," she said, in a thick Romany accent. "Please sit down and cross my palm with silver – or a ha'penny. Whatever you can afford." I giggled and gave her a sixpence. She did some curious hand movements over the snow globe – crystal ball – and muttered an incantation about the spirits giving her foresight or something. "I see a man who is close to you. One who has always loved you." I must admit it was all rather affecting and I forgot for a moment that it was Anne behind the mask.

"Really?" I said, wondering who it could be. "I don't think my husband would like that." I must admit I rather liked the idea of having a secret admirer.

"Perhaps," she said. "The love of your life is closer than you know."

It still did not ring any bells for me.

"Perhaps…" She sounded a bit impatient. "He is hiding within plain sight."

Still nothing came to mind. But it was all very silly, anyway. I thanked her and left. Emma Carstairs went in next and apparently she was told the very same thing.

"We'll have to make a list of likely candidates," Emma said, smiling. I could not help feeling she was not taking it seriously, but I spent the rest of the afternoon wondering who my secret admirer was.

It was late in the day when I saw Guy Marsh go into the tent. He was in there much longer than anyone else was, and I wondered what she was telling him. She probably told him to pretend he was in love with me and Emma, knowing the sort of person she has turned out to be!

Guy was still in the tent when his stepbrother, the Detective Inspector arrived. "Is Anne Pargeter here?" Andrew Marsh asked, strolling across the grass to meet me.

"Yes, she's in the fortune telling tent, giving Group Captain Marsh a reading."

"Thank you, Mrs Sullivan."

The detective went into the tent with two of his men, and a few moments later, they came out with Anne. What's more, she was wearing handcuffs...

Group Captain Guy Marsh

I don't think I admitted to myself just how much in love I was with Anne Pargeter until the day of the garden party. She had told me that it was her intention to make everyone happy, but I didn't realise how committed she was to that promise until she brought out the wheelchairs for the final race. It was her intention to ensure that our young friend, Hotspur, had his moment in the spotlight.

As I took the last wheelchair, she walked across to me and leaned over, her subtle perfume filling my head with sensual thoughts I cannot repeat here. "Don't you dare try to win," she whispered.

"That'll cost you a kiss," I said. She moved away, laughing, but she had not said no.

I don't think I could have won if I'd tried. Those wheelchairs were unwieldy to say the least. I got so far up the track, and then fell into a pothole out of which I could not extricate myself. I finally ended up going around in circles as young Hotspur stole the race.

I had never seen that kid so happy. His smile was even wider when young Jennifer treated him like a conquering hero. Young love is probably the best sort of love there is. It leaves no room for doubts or insecurities. They may not be together the rest of their lives, but at that age, one year is an eternity, and I wished them every joy in that time; no doubt because I was in a silly romantic mood myself.

Anne had pitched the day just right. I wanted to tell her so, but she disappeared. I think it was Emma Carstairs who told me that Anne was to be *Madame Fortuna* for the afternoon. I waited for a suitable gap in the proceedings, before entering the tent.

Incense and exotic aromas filled the air. Anne sat on one side of the table, looking like Scheherazade in a silk veil that covered her lower face, and thick black kohl which accentuated her green eyes. I don't know if I imagined that she looked startled when I walked in. I know we had not spoken much since the trip to Flamborough Head. I know for certain that she was avoiding me, but apart from meal times when others were around, we had not been alone together and I couldn't help wondering if she had arranged things that way.

"I can't decide whether to ask you to tell me a story or my fortune," I said.

"It depends if you intend to chop my head off in the morning." She spoke in a Romany accent, showing a great talent for mimicry. "Cross my palm with silver."

I handed over my sixpence and our hands touched slightly. "That was a really good thing that you did for our young friend, Hotspur."

"Shh," she said. "That was someone else."

"Saint Anne?" I quipped.

"Yes. Something like that."

She waved her hands around the crystal ball. "The crystal ball sees all."

"It seems to be telling us that we're going to have a

white Christmas, and that Santa and Rudolph will be visiting," I said. Her eyes twinkled and I imagined that under the veil her lips curved up at the corners.

"Not everything is as it seems," she said in more serious tones. "Not everyone is as they seem. There is a viper in the picnic basket." I had no idea then that she was talking about herself. "You would be better to keep your distance."

"From you?"

"I am Madame Fortuna," she chided.

"From Saint Anne then?"

"Perhaps…"

I caught her by the wrist. "Why, Anne? Why must I keep away? What did I say in Filey to put you off? Is it because my father was murdered? I know that some people don't like to be caught up in such things."

"That does not bother me…her…"

I reached up and pulled the veil from her face. "Stop this. Stop trying to put me off. I'm in love with you, can't you see?"

"Yes, I can see," she said, her eyes filling with tears. She looked into the crystal ball as if she would find answers in its icy landscape. "But I can see only heartache for us."

I stood up and pulled her into my arms, kissing her as if both our lives depended upon it. She clung to me, her hand caressing my cheek, but I tasted tears in the kiss we shared.

"What is it, darling?" I asked when we finally drew breath. "Whatever you've done, or think you've done, it won't matter as long as we're together." My hasty promise came back to mock me when I found out the truth only a few moments later.

"It will matter," she whispered. "Some things are insurmountable, no matter how much we wish they weren't. I just want you to know how much I've enjoyed being with you this summer. I love you, Guy. But we cannot be together."

103

As if on cue, the tent flap opened and I looked to see my stepbrother entering. "Andrew?"

"Guy, I need you to step aside."

"Why? What are you doing?" I guessed he had come to see Anne, but I could think of no reason why. "She has done nothing wrong."

"Guy, please," Andrew said. "Don't make this harder than it is."

Anne extricated herself from my arms and put as much distance as possible between us, given the confines of the tent. "It's alright," she said. "I know why you've come, Detective Inspector. I've been waiting for this for a long time."

"Mary-Ann Lakeham." My stepbrother spoke in official tones, but even then the name did not set off any alarm bells in my head. "We would like to speak to you in relation to the deaths of George Peterson and Bunty Lemington-Smith."

"What?" I looked from Anne to Andrew then back again. "Her name is Anne Pargeter."

"It isn't," she said. "I'm sorry, Guy. I've lied to everyone. I'm Mary-Ann Lakeham and my mother was Eleanor Grace."

"You…you killed my father?"

It is a strange thing, the love of a parent. You can spend a good part of your life convincing yourself that an absent father means nothing to you. That it is better that he is dead, because he was a waste of oxygen anyway. But when faced with the woman who was suspected of bringing about his death, blood reigns supreme, and bitter thoughts of vengeance break through. "Tell me it isn't true," I insisted somewhat half-heartedly because I knew that it must be if Andrew was there. My stepbrother did not make mistakes.

"I…I can't." Anne bowed her head and allowed my stepbrother and his men to put her in handcuffs and lead her from the tent.

Percy Sullivan

It was awful. The worst day of my life. Until then it had been the best day. I had beaten everyone else in the wheelchair race, including Group Captain Marsh. Jennifer thought I was brilliant. Afterwards we had ice lollies, and a go on the shooting games. I won her a ragdoll which she said she would keep always.

Then we heard people murmuring and saw them all looking towards the fortune telling tent. They brought Anne out, in handcuffs.

"Quickly, Jennifer, help me to get to her," I cried, throwing down the candy floss I had been eating. Jennifer turned out to be really good at pushing the wheelchair through crowds though I think she might have banged a few ankles on the way.

"Anne!" I cried. "Anne, where are you going?"

She had been walking with the police till then, but she stopped and looked at me and then at the Group Captain. "Oh, Percy," she said, starting to cry. "No matter what anyone tells you, it wasn't all lies. I want you to believe that. Now don't watch, darling. Please don't watch."

I think I might have started to cry then. I know Mother came across and then Henry had to carry me up to bed, because I made such a fuss and told everyone to bugger off. I don't suppose Jennifer liked me very much after that. I don't really know, because the house party sort of broke up then and everyone went back home, including us.

I saw the ghost again, even though no one believes me. She was standing in the corridor near to my room on the day they took Anne. Henry had me thrown over his shoulder, because I was screaming so much, and thumping him in the back.

"Hush, little one," she said. "All will be well."

"Henry, look it's the ghost," I said. He turned around, nearly hitting my head on the wall, which halted his progress a bit. He asked where. "There, right in the corridor," I said. He turned again, so I should have been facing the ghost, but she had gone.

They brought Doctor Aitken to me, and he gave me a sedative with a needle. "Terrible business," he said. "Who'd have thought such a nice girl would come to such a bad end?"

"She's not a criminal," I said. "She's not."

"There, there, lad. I know you had a soft spot for young Anne."

I wanted to tell him that I didn't like Anne in that way. Not the way I liked Jennifer. But Anne was a good egg. She looked after all us, and I think she helped Mother to relax more. But my mouth got all dry and I couldn't say anything, before everything went black and I think I must have slept.

Detective Inspector Andrew Marsh

Mary-Ann Lakeham (aka Anne Pargeter) put up no resistance at all when we arrested her. She spoke to young Percy Sullivan but she did not say a word to us. We took her to the local police station for initial questioning, and then moved her to London when she had been put before the magistrate.

During questioning she put up no defence, only answering 'Yes' quietly when asked if she understood the charges against her. We could get nothing else out of her. When we asked her why she had killed two people, she refused to answer. Then, when asked by the magistrate how she pleaded, she replied, "Guilty."

Whilst we at the Yard were glad to have finally solved two murders, we were a little disappointed at her reaction to being arrested. We had hoped for some explanation. We knew that if she carried on her guilty plea to the courts, then we might never find out why a seemingly capable and level-headed young woman decided to murder two innocent people.

I have visited her several times, as have several of our top criminologists, but she refuses to cooperate. We have no means of encouraging or threatening her to give us the information we need. She is going to be hanged. In short she has nothing left to lose and we have nothing with which to bargain.

Anne Pargeter

Dearest Hotspur,

You know the truth about me now. I am sure that whatever information is missing has been filled in by the newspapers. They seem to know things about me that even I do not know.

My mother was the actress, Eleanor Grace, formerly Helen Pargeter. She was born in Derbyshire, and when she was just sixteen years old, she married a man called John Lakeham, who was a few years older. He was the heir to Lakeham Abbey, and they moved there soon after their marriage. They had been together only a short time, and my mother was still expecting me, when she realised she had married a man who was quite mad. My father was given to psychotic rages and periods of great depression. When he attacked one of the villagers in a drunken fury he was committed to an asylum. They had known each other less than six months. My mother was told by my father's family that she was no longer welcome in Lakeham Abbey.

My mother changed her name to Eleanor Grace and managed to find regular work in the theatre. In a very short time she became one of the most celebrated actresses of her era. She was helped by Maudie, an old friend whom Mother often turned to when she was alone and frightened. Maudie cared for me whilst Mother worked.

Eventually, my father died in the asylum and I was the heir to Lakeham Abbey, despite the family trying to claim otherwise. I don't know what made Mother move us back there, after her terrible experience. Perhaps she did it for my sake.

The newspapers have covered all my mother's love affairs. I admit to remembering several 'uncles' coming into our lives, but my mother was still very young, beautiful and full of life. Fate had dealt her a bad hand in the shape of a violent, deranged husband. So she sought happiness and acceptance where she could. I cannot condemn her for seeking comfort with other men, even if those romances were of the fleeting variety.

I remember George Peterson well. I think I was about twelve when he came into Mother's life. I know what the newspapers have said about him too, and I understand that he was not the best of husbands and fathers. All I can say is that when I met him, I truly believed that he loved my mother. He also treated me with kindness and respect, which I'm ashamed to say, is more than I showed to him. He often spoke of his son, George, and how he wished they were not estranged. I think he was a man who had made mistakes but was ready to settle down with the one woman he loved. I did not see it that way, and was not always kind or fair to him. I had not behaved the same way with my mother's other lovers, but I think that I knew those romances were always going to be brief. I began to realise that George Peterson was going to become a permanent fixture in our lives and I was not happy about it.

How could I have known then that his son would be the man to whom I would give my heart?

It is difficult to talk about the night George Peterson died without explaining some of the problems leading up to it. Despite all her experiences and the fact she was an actress, my mother was normally a sensible woman. Yet, for several months she began to feel that she – all of us in fact – were being watched.

Strange things happened in that house. Locked doors, whose keys had long since gone missing, would be found open. There would be dirty footprints running through the scullery (much to Maudie's chagrin). Windows would fly open, as if the catches had been worn loose.

At first, Peterson would laugh about the 'ghost'. But

as Mother became more concerned, and expressed fear that my father had somehow returned to harm us, we both began to worry more. Strangely, it brought Peterson and me a little closer. I may not have liked him, but we both loved my mother, so we became united in our wish to make her happy.

We went to see Doctor Aitken. I recognised him immediately when I came back to Lakeham with the Sullivans, but he did not recognise me. A kindly man, albeit a bit of a gossip about his rich patients, he had been my father's physician before he was committed to the asylum, and the good doctor began to take care of my mother. For a short time she seemed to improve, and she and George talked about getting married.

Until that last awful night. There was a storm, and it was as if the house came alive. Doors banged, windows rattled, shutters creaked. Every sound made us jump. Mother was tearful, Peterson was irritable. I was just pensive, sensing that something awful was going to happen. It had been a feeling growing within me for several months. In many ways, I became as skittish as my mother, jumping at every sound.

Eventually, tensions became so heightened that we had a huge bust up. Peterson called me a 'spoiled brat'. I called him a 'freeloader', living off my money (it shames me to remember that as he had never asked Mother for anything). Mother, poor dear, was caught between us both. Oh, how dramatic I was when I was thirteen.

"You have to choose. Him or me," I cried, flouncing from the room.

You know now the facts of the case. George Peterson was found dead on the very same terrace on which we found Bunty Lemington-Smith, having fallen from the roof.

I know you cannot understand, dearest Hotspur, why I have pleaded guilty to both crimes. Love is a very strange thing. When you love two people and have to make a choice of which one to save, it can be very difficult. One is torn hither and thither, until it feels as if your very soul will tear in two.

I saw the look of hatred in Guy's eyes when he realised who I was. He has no doubt that I had killed his father. None at all. Since my arrest he has made no effort to believe in my innocence, nor lifted a finger to try to save me.

This makes it much easier for me to save another that I love, even if to do that I have to go all the way to hell.

I just wish I had never met you and Lily. I do love you both dearly, and now my soul is torn in two again. Please understand that I must do this and there is nothing that you can do to stop it.

Your friend,
Anne Pargeter

Jennifer Carstairs
Age 14

Hello Percy. Stop. Daddy got your letter. Stop. Mummy is coming back next week to see new house. Stop. I'm coming out of school for a week to see her. Stop. Ask your mother if you can come for a visit. Stop. We can solve this together. Stop.

Chapter Eight

Percy Sullivan

Mother and Father did not want me to go to Jennifer's house. I don't think they wanted me to go back to Lakeham Abbey and they probably suspected that's what we were up to. I had to promise – with my fingers crossed – that I would not go near to the place.

They insisted Henry come with me, which made things a bit difficult, but Jennifer assured me that she had a plan.

"We'll pretend we're boyfriend and girlfriend and want to be left alone," she said.

"Henry won't fall for that."

"Why ever not?"

"Because boys like me don't get girlfriends like you."

"Oh, you are silly sometimes, Hotspur," Jennifer laughed. She had never called me that before. Did it mean that she saw me as a close friend? Or was she teasing me because that's what Anne and Guy called me?

Mother cried when she saw me off on the train. We had been spending a lot of what she called Quality Time together, but to be honest, it was getting a bit stifling. I am quite fond of Mother, of course, but after years of being neglected (ignored, unloved) by her and having to occupy myself, I wasn't sure I liked having her around me all the time.

"I have a feeling something awful will happen," she said, as she kissed me goodbye.

"Mother, I'm perfectly capable of taking care of myself," I said, trying to sound very mature. "Henry is with me."

"Don't let him near that awful house," Mother said to Henry. He nodded in agreement.

Jennifer and her mother met me at the other end and drove us to their house in the village near to Lakeham Abbey. I like Mrs Carstairs. She's very calm and doesn't fuss like Mother does.

"How are you, Percy?" she asked.

"I'm very well, thank you, Mrs Carstairs. Thank you for inviting me." Even though I was tired and achy, I thought I'd better be polite and not swear at her, in case she put me on the next train home.

"I like your house," I said to Jennifer, when she rolled my wheelchair up the garden path (she told me we had to start as we meant to go on, by her taking over from Henry as much as possible). Her mother and Henry followed us. I think Mrs Carstairs was telling him about our sleeping arrangements as I heard her say something about an adjoining room. "It's much nicer than our poky little flat," I said. The garden was a bit too flowery for my liking, but I think Mother and Lily would have liked it. The house was long and white, with a couple of apex roofs, and Tudor style beams crossing the white sections.

"It is rather nice," she agreed. "Me and Mummy love it, but Daddy hardly ever comes here."

"Jennifer…" Mrs Carstairs said. It was like she was warning Jennifer about something.

"Is he still abroad?" I asked.

"Yes," said Mrs Carstairs, before Jennifer could answer. "There's some trouble in the Middle East and Angus is involved in negotiations. I was there, but Jennifer missed me so I came home, didn't I, darling?"

"Yes, Mummy."

I don't really understand much about what goes on between grown-ups, but I'd heard Mother sounding just as careful when she and Father had an argument.

After lunch, Jennifer took me for a look at the village. All the time I'd stayed at Lakeham Abbey I hardly left the grounds, apart from the trip to Harley Street. We went into the sweet shop and used up all our sweet rations. We couldn't talk for a while, as we sucked on our gobstoppers, so Jennifer just pushed me to the village side of the lake, where we sat and looked across at the Abbey.

I hoped we would see the ghost at the window, but we were too far away. We could only see the sky reflected in the glass. I began to wonder if Anne had been correct and that was all we had seen the first time. To be honest, the idea of a ghost was beginning to sound silly to me. I'd only been a child last time we were there. Now I was a whole year older.

"How do we get in?" I asked when my gobstopper had shrunk a bit.

"Easy," she replied through a mouthful of sweets. "There is a skeleton staff, just going in to turn over the beds once or twice a week, so no one is really watching it. All we do is walk up to the door and if it's open, go in. I tried it the other day, and managed to get all the way up to the nursery and back out without being seen. If anyone sees us, we can say we've stayed there before and that we left something behind."

"Like what?"

"Like the baby doll I left when I went there the other day." Jennifer grinned. Her teeth had gone a funny blue colour. "I thought we could say it was Lily's."

"You're really clever for a girl."

"Girls are cleverer than boys. We just have to pretend not to be. Mummy said it upsets the male ego." Jennifer fell silent then and I wondered if what I said had really upset her.

"Sorry," I said after a bit. "I didn't mean to be rude."

"It's not you," Jennifer said. "It's Mummy and Daddy. You mustn't say anything, but they're getting a divorce."

"Oh." Hardly anyone we knew were divorced, apart from the Duchess of Windsor, and no one in Britain liked her because she made our king abdicate. "That's tough on you."

"Yes, I know. I shall be an underprivileged child and none of the girls at school will want to talk to me."

"Underprivileged?"

"Yes, Daddy said that if Mummy divorces him, he'll take the house and everything. We will probably have to go on the dole. And wear clogs."

"Is clog wearing compulsory for people on the dole?"

"I think it might be. And owning a whippet."

"I should rather like a whippet. Mother won't let us have a dog, because we live in the flat. So if you get a whippet, I can help you to take care of it. And I'm sure my mother and father will still invite your mother to dinner, so you can eat a couple of times a week."

"Oh, do you think so?" She stood up and kissed me on the forehead. "You are rather sweet sometimes, Hotspur. When you're not being grumpy about your legs."

"You'd be grumpy if you had my useless legs, Jennifer."

"Oh, I wouldn't. I'd be rather brave, I should think, and bear my affliction with grace. Like Saint Bernadette."

I didn't want to speak to her then. Her words wounded me. She obviously thought I was a coward. I couldn't really blame her. I had been no help at all when she was trapped on the upper floor with someone about to find her. I wished I could bear my affliction with grace, but the truth was that my spine and legs blooming hurt most of the time.

"You've gone quiet, Hotspur." She looked at me from under her lashes.

"I'm thinking more." I didn't even know what that meant but it was something Henry often said.

"Thinking about what?"

"Nothing. The investigation. That's all. I think we should go back now."

When we got back to Jennifer's house, we found that

her father had returned. He was sitting in the garden with her mother. I recognised the tight smiles on their faces from times when my parents argued but wanted to pretend that everything was alright.

"Fetch Henry," I said to Jennifer. "I'd like to go and rest."

"Would it hurt you to say please?"

"Please."

She flounced off; unaware of what she had said to hurt me. Which made it hurt all the more. She should have known. Why did she always think she could be better at doing things than anyone else?

Feeling uncomfortable with her parents, I moved my wheelchair around the corner. As I did, I heard her father say, "You lied to me, Emma. But I'm willing to forgive you."

"How magnanimous of you," said Mrs Carstairs. "This has nothing to do with you keeping your seat in Parliament, I suppose."

"I just thought that," Mr Carstairs said, "now that Bunty Lemington-Smith is dead, no one else will ever know. Least of all Jennifer."

Celia Sullivan

I don't know why I felt anxious about letting Percy go to Jennifer's. I'd often waved him off as he went to boarding school. This felt different. This trip involved his heart, and I feared that she would break it. Jennifer Carstairs will soon be a very beautiful young woman. She is already full of vitality. She won't want to tie herself to a boy in a wheelchair for her whole life.

Believe me when I say I feel no animosity towards her for that. It is a big commitment for any girl, let alone one of fourteen. I do feel concerned for my boy and his future. What will happen to him when we are no longer here to take care of him? Who will love him as we do?

All this was on my mind when I returned home from the station. Freddie was off on some seminar, so it was just Lily and me. She wanted to play hairdressers, so my hair was rather a mess when I heard the doorbell. I opened it to find Guy Marsh.

"I'm going back to Lakeham Abbey to investigate," he said, before he had even said hello. He looked a little unkempt himself. His face was pale and he had dark rings under his eyes. "The thing is, I have no right to be there. So I wondered if you wanted to come with me."

"Why me?"

"You stayed in the house. You could pretend you left something there."

"Oh, I see. Yes, I suppose so. What do you want to investigate? Surely the case is all finished. Anne Pargeter will be executed soon." I noticed he winced when I said that.

"I just want to be sure it was her. For my own peace of mind."

"Are you doubting her guilt?" A shiver ran through me. I had come to realise that if it was found that Anne had not killed Bunty, then the police would look for someone else among the house party.

"No. Yes. No. See what that bloody woman has done to me?" He ran his hands through his hair. "I'm normally so sure about everything. Then I went to see her in prison. I saw the hurt in her eyes when I didn't believe in her innocence. It could all be an act. She could have learned a lot about acting from her mother. But until I've investigated this properly, I won't know. So I want to speak to people in the area. Those who lived there at the time of my father's murder. They may know something that the police have missed. And I need to get into that house. Are you coming with me or not, Celia?"

"I will come, if you tell me the truth about something."

"What's that?"

"Why did you invite yourself to stay? Doctor Aitken saw you talking to your brother in town before the murder. Why was he there?"

He took a deep breath. "Very well. I'll tell you on the way."

Professor Freddie Sullivan

It was most irregular. I came back from the seminar early. I thought that with Percy away and Lily in bed early, Celia and I might spend some time together. It was hard to find privacy in our small flat, with two rather demanding children. Do not misunderstand me. I love my son and my daughter. But I do sometimes wish I had my wife all to myself.

When I got home I found a note from Celia.

'Freddie,
Gone back to Lakeham to investigate with Guy. Taken Lily with me. We may be gone several days. There's a tin of soup and some Spam in the cupboard.
Love
Celia'

It was not good enough. A man likes to know his wife can be relied upon. Yet here she was, off on some jaunt with Guy Marsh. Of course, he was nearer to her age. Younger in fact, which made me think she was behaving rather foolishly. I saw some relief in that. It could be her age. Women get a bit silly in their late thirties. She may yet get over him and come back to me.

What if she did not? I had long since known that I had married a woman far superior to myself in terms of looks and charm. I'm a dry old stick. But I did believe that Celia loved me when we married.

Now I begin to wonder. When we married, I think she was only trying to escape Bunty Lemington-Smith. That woman cast a shadow over our lives for too long, with her possessiveness towards Celia and the way she liked to think she had something against every one of us. Bunty was a muckraker, digging around in other people's cupboards to unearth the skeletons lying there.

117

It gave her a feeling of superiority when her own life was so very small and petty. If she had married and had children, perhaps she would have been different. A husband and children bring meaning to a woman's life.

My only other fear is what else Celia and Guy might uncover when they get to Lakeham. I think we covered our tracks quite well, but there are always difficulties with these things. Bunty worked out what was going on. She confronted me with it on the night she died. She wanted money to stay silent.

"I'm sure Celia would not be too happy with what you're up to," she told me. "I'm broke, Freddie. I've overstretched myself with the gallery. It was only a vanity project anyway, but I owe people money."

"Why come to me?" I asked. "You hate me."

"This is why I came to you. I'd hardly blackmail someone I cared about. I need three hundred pounds. I'm sure you can afford it, for all you look as if you've bought your clothes at a thrift shop."

"They're not second hand clothes. They're just rather old. There has been a war on, Bunty."

"I'm sure you can afford better in your new line of business."

She put me in a difficult situation. If the truth came out, it would not just be me who suffered. But I did not have three hundred pounds, and it was an amount I could not even go to my cousin, the Duke of Marsholm with, even if his own name might be dragged through the mud.

It was rather lucky that Bunty died when she did.

Guy Marsh

There had been hints that Freddie Sullivan and his academic friends were up to something for a while. During the war, many works of art, including Van Gogh's self-portrait *Painter on His Way to Work*, and Caravaggio's *Saint Matthew and the Angel*, were destroyed by fire. Other important artefacts, like the

Amber Room from St Petersburg – a rococo room built in amber and gold, was dismantled by the Nazis, but then disappeared, assumed lost at sea. It seemed a fair bet that some of the Nazis still had these artefacts and had probably used them to start a new life in South America.

It was easy, then, for other smugglers and black marketers to take artefacts and sell them to private collectors, letting the world believe that they had been lost or destroyed during the chaos of war.

My stepbrother, Andrew, was involved in an investigation into a suspected smuggling ring that had collected works from Eastern Europe before the Iron Curtain closed off all routes, bringing them to Britain, presumably to sell to collectors. The Soviet authorities, through the Soviet Embassy, were demanding that the British authorities investigate the theft of art that they believed belonged to them.

"Personally, I couldn't care less about the communists losing their treasures," Andrew had told me when he met me in a pub before I went to Lakeham. "They're not supposed to care about that sort of thing anyway. You have no idea how much art they looted themselves during the war. But the powers that be are insisting we at least look as if we're doing something."

"And you think Freddie Sullivan is involved?"

"He has links to two men we've been watching. They're known only as Sergei and Ivan. Go down there, Guy. See what you can find out."

"Freddie is family, Andrew."

"I know."

"And you still want me to investigate him?"

"We have to be seen to be impartial."

"Will he go to prison? What if the Soviets want him?"

"We'll do our best to ensure that doesn't happen, Guy. Look, I'm not asking you to be Sherlock Holmes. All we need is to be seen to be doing something. You send me reports that I can show to the Soviets. With any luck it will appease them. You'll be paid for your trouble. I'll see to that."

I couldn't turn that down. Work had been scarce since the war ended. I was slowly building my air freight business, but the plane often cost more money to fly than I earned and I had rent to pay. I could have done a bit of smuggling myself and solved all my problems, but I wanted to at least try to stay on the right side of the law.

So I snagged an invitation to Lakeham Abbey, all the while hating myself for spying on a relative. I did as Andrew suggested; the least amount possible, whilst sending in tepid reports about nothing really happening. I even managed to be absent for most of the evening when Sergei and Ivan stayed for dinner. They seemed to be decent enough men. Certainly not gangsters or hoodlums. I honestly didn't care if they were stealing art from Eastern Europe.

As Andrew had said, the Soviets did enough of their own looting during the war. It seemed to me that all they wanted was to maximise the profits of their annexation of Eastern Europe by grabbing as much as they could. What did Joseph Conrad call the colonisation of Africa? A vile scramble for loot? The Soviet government was not above such tactics themselves. Some people truly were more equal than others when it came to dividing the spoils of war.

I was, however, intrigued by Freddie's part in it all. He did not appear to be any richer than normal. In fact, I'd have said finances were rather tight for the Sullivans. I know, from things that Celia said, that our cousin, the Duke of Marsholm, paid young Hotspur's school fees and had promised to pay Lily's. So whether the smugglers had not yet paid Freddie for his help, or if he was doing it just for the thrill, I did not know. He appeared to be his usual, unassuming and rather boring self.

I was also confused by how this artwork was being moved around. A few old Etruscan pots were not exactly the same as paintings or sculptures. As far as I could see, no outlandishly large crates were ever delivered to the Abbey. I did see a few sugar crates, but that was all.

All this I explained to Celia as we drove down to Lakeham. I had left the plane behind this time, because of the little girl coming with us.

"I'm sorry, Celia," I said. "I will understand if you never want to speak to me again."

"Freddie, involved with smugglers?" She looked at me with the wide, innocent eyes of a child. "Surely not. Oh, but you are naughty, Guy. We trusted you."

"I know, and you still can trust me. I've sent in a report to the Soviets that is benign in the extreme, talking about the picnics and garden parties. They'll think we're a bunch of Neros, fiddling whilst Rome burns, so they'll be delighted that capitalism is as bad as they believe. But they won't pin anything on Freddie. Anne's arrest also helped take the focus off the smuggling. Andrew has been able to tell the Soviets that we've other, more important, fish to fry." I shuddered at my own words. As if Anne's pending execution were a convenient way of ensuring Freddie and his smuggling friends did not get into trouble.

"Guy?"

"What?"

"Do you think it's possible that Bunty found out about the smuggling? She had a way of knowing things that people didn't want her to know."

"Yes, I suppose it is. What are you saying? That someone else might have killed her?"

"Oh, no," Celia said hastily. "It must have been Anne who killed her, mustn't it? She was the one with the motive."

"Yes, it must have been."

"So why are we investigating?"

"To make sure," I said. Because of the sadness in her eyes when I saw her in the prison. Because I had to be sure she was not fooling me with some act she had

121

learned from her mother. Because I was still in love with her and the only way to free myself of that curse was to prove once and for all that she had murdered both my father and Bunty Lemington-Smith.

"The fact is," Andrew told me, after Anne was sentenced, "we have no evidence to prove any of it. We only have Anne Pargeter's confession and guilty plea. I for one would prefer to have a lot more proof, just in case she ever decides to recant and gets herself a barrister who actually cares about her case."

It was fair to say that the barrister assigned to her only did the bare minimum. What else could he do for a woman who had pleaded guilty? He could have fought harder for her, a quiet uneasy voice in my head replied. We could have all fought harder for her, but none of us did.

When young Hotspur sent me copies of all the testimonies he had amassed, Anne's death sentence was convenient to so many of those who had been there that summer. Celia Sullivan, who had her own reasons for wanting Bunty dead; Freddie Sullivan, who was up to his neck with the smugglers; the smugglers themselves; and the Carstairs, who, according to Doctor Aitken's testimony, had their own secrets that Bunty threatened to expose. I was the only one with no reason to kill Bunty, which in a crime novel would make me the prime suspect.

Anne had been the one with the biggest motive. She had, she said, killed my father, and Bunty had somehow found out. So Anne had killed Bunty to silence her. Not that Anne had said any of this. She had simply pleaded guilty. We had to guess the rest.

Celia and I booked into a hotel in the countryside. She did not want to go into Lakeham village too often. "Percy is staying there with Jennifer," she explained. "It wouldn't do for him to see me. I told him to keep away from Lakeham Abbey."

We did not get started that afternoon. Young Lily

needed a nap, and by the time we had eaten dinner it was too late to set out.

It was the morning before we could go anywhere. I had found out the name of someone who had worked at the Abbey during the time that Eleanor Grace lived there and my father was murdered. Her name was Mrs Turner. She had retired to a cottage on the edge of the village.

We sat amongst dozens of knick-knacks and photographs of Mrs Turner as a young woman, with Mr Turner, who had apparently been in service at the same time. He had died before the war.

"I worked in the kitchen," she explained. "It was a strange sort of affair." She sniffed. Servants were usually a little bit put out by upper class morality. "They weren't married. Did you say you were related to him?" She glanced at me suspiciously, as if she feared I would do something immoral in her house.

"He was my father."

"Oh. I see."

"He and my mother were married," I added, with an edge to my voice. "He left us."

"Very sad for you, I'm sure, though I don't hold with all this divorce. Together over twenty years, me and Mr Turner were. So what if he did drink and chat up the barmaid in the pub? My mother said to me, 'You made your bed, you lie on it, girl'. So we stuck together." She sniffed again. "That's how murders happen."

"What?" Celia frowned. "When you don't make your bed?"

"No, when a man doesn't live up to his responsibilities."

"Are you suggesting that my father deserved to be murdered?" I asked.

"No, I don't say that. Only that if someone gets involved in immoral goings on, there's no telling what will happen."

"What can you tell us about Mary-Ann Lakeham?" I asked. I thought I would explode, sitting in that room with that small-minded woman. Odd, how I had disapproved of my father all my life, yet did not like to hear her pronounce judgement on him.

"The daughter? The one who's been done for his murder? Well, it's not surprising she turned out to be a murderer, is it? Not with her family background."

"Did she get on with my father?"

"No, not really. Not at first, anyway. They got friendlier when her mother became poorly. There's madness in that family. Her father was carted off to an asylum, you know."

"Were you there then?" Celia asked.

"No, I wasn't. But I heard about it from my friend, Mrs Williams. She used to work there when Eleanor Grace first got married to Sir Henry's son, John. He had to be locked up after he attacked someone in the pub. No doubt his daughter has inherited his murderous ways."

"There's a difference between beating someone up and murdering them." I don't know why I was defending Anne. I think it was because I didn't like Mrs Turner's particular brand of morality, which seemed to revel in misfortune and hellfire even for those who may only be associated with the sins of others. If Anne's father was ill, then he might not be responsible for his actions. And then she might not be responsible for hers…

I dispensed with that thought. She had killed my father. That was something I could never accept, even if she was mentally incapacitated at the time.

"Do you know the man he attacked?" Celia asked Mrs Turner.

"Why no, but Doctor Aitken might."

"Doctor Aitken?"

"Yes, he was the Lakeham's doctor at the time. It was he who had Mr Lakeham committed."

I almost laughed. We had been talking to the wrong person when all the time our friend, Doctor Aitken, was in a much better, and more reliable, position to tell us what had happened.

Doctor Aitken

It was a terrible business. Terrible. Mrs Lakeham was very young. Not much older than sixteen or seventeen if I remember correctly. With her long golden hair and innocent face, she reminded me of the painting by Frank Cadogan Cowper, which shows Lucretia Borgia sitting high on a throne whilst a Franciscan friar kisses her feet. A lot of men would have been happy to kiss young Helen's feet.

John Lakeham was a few years older and had been running with a rough crowd in London before he met his wife. The couple had what is known as a whirlwind romance.

John's mother and father had died when he was in school, but he had several aunts and uncles who took a proprietary interest in him. It is incumbent upon me to point out that if John Lakeham died without issue, the Abbey would pass to one of his cousins. So you can imagine their chagrin when he upped and married at a time they had all assumed he was going to become untouchable for any woman, due to his wild lifestyle. The family were also rather snobbish. The girl, as charming as she was to everyone who met her, was not from the same class.

I believe they were happy at first. I saw John from time to time, as he battled the demons left over from his wild days. He had seen me before about an addiction to heroin. I believed he had beaten that, with my help. Sadly, he soon became plagued with anxiety and nerves. He told me that he suffered nightmares and had started to see things. He also feared he might harm his young wife.

"I nearly slapped her yesterday, and yet she had said or done nothing to warrant it," he confided in me. "I'm afraid, Aitken. She is expecting a baby. What if I harm her?"

I knew that the family would be very disturbed by the news, but of course patient confidentiality is one of my

125

strictest tenets. I can only discuss John Lakeham now because he is dead.

I went straight to see Helen, because I was concerned for her welfare. Of course I did not discuss what John had told me. I merely visited as a friend. I found the dear young girl terrified, which is not a good thing for an expectant mother.

I examined her and found her to be strong, and the baby to be healthy. I did wonder what might happen to the baby if she became too distressed.

"I know John is a good man, despite his mistakes," she told me. "But sometimes I fear his temper. Help me to help him, Doctor Aitken."

I promised that I would help her in any way possible. It was clear she still loved her husband, but it seemed to me that if he were to behave cruelly towards her and their unborn child, that love might die.

Then came the fateful day we had to commit him to the asylum. He had taken some concoction that gave him severe hallucinations and paranoia. He began to suspect everyone of plotting against him and spoke to me about the men he felt sure were going to take him away from his family.

Yet he still did not harm his young wife. Perhaps some inner sense of morality prevented it, despite his condition. Who can fathom the human mind?

One evening, he left his wife resting in her room whilst he went to the local pub. He told us later that he was supposed to meet someone there, but no note or message was ever discovered. Some thug approached John Lakeham and began to abuse him about his position in life. The thug had just got out of prison, so was at odds with the world. I am told that at first John resisted the man's attempts to start a fight.

"I don't want any trouble," he told the man. "I am just here to meet someone."

The lowlife – I forget the man's name – kept goading him, until finally he cast aspersions on the morality of

John's lovely young wife. At that point, I am told, John became hostile. At first he merely shouted at the man, and warned him to keep his mouth shut. The man ignored that, calling Helen Lakeham a slut and a whore, and suggesting that the baby she carried was not John's.

There was a bottle of whisky on the bar. I do not know who had bought it. But spectators say that John caught it and smashed it, going for his abuser like a man possessed. Several men had to pull John off him, and the man barely escaped with his life. He threatened to call the police, to have John imprisoned.

That was when I happened to walk into the pub and learn what had happened. I helped John back to his house where I gave him a sedative. I had no choice, for John and his wife's sake, but to ask a fellow doctor to co-sign a letter of committal to the asylum.

"It is the only way he can escape the police," I explained to a distraught Helen. "But we will soon have him out of there."

She took it surprisingly well, nodding her agreement. "I just want the man I love back," she told me. She must have been made of stronger stuff than I thought, as she and the baby survived the ordeal.

John did not survive. He died in the asylum several months later. Somehow he got hold of a razor blade and cut his own throat.

It was a sorry business all round. Helen went away and I did not see her for many years, except at the cinema along with anyone else who could pay the entrance fee. She finally returned to Lakeham Abbey some years later. With her she brought her lover, George Peterson, and her daughter, Mary-Ann, who had inherited the house. I wondered then if the girl had also inherited her father's insanity.

There is no doubt in my mind that she did, even if she did not plead insanity during her trial.

Celia Sullivan

I must say I quite enjoyed being an investigator alongside Guy Marsh. I was rather hampered by having to take Lily everywhere with us, but she is a good little girl and often played happily while we talked to people. And I am proud to say I never forgot about her once, even if we were very busy.

My only concern was that I was not sure exactly what Guy wanted to prove. Did he want Anne to be innocent or guilty? He played his cards very close to his chest and kept any feelings he might have for her a secret from me.

Speaking for myself, I did not know what to think. She had admitted her guilt and yet the Anne I knew had been kind and helpful. Perhaps it was true about the madness in her family, in which case she cannot help what she is and I am very sorry for her.

When Doctor Aitken could not tell us the name of the man that Anne's father had attacked, Guy suggested we go to the local pub and ask around.

"Do you think they'll remember a fight that happened some thirty years ago?" I asked. "Surely such places have fights all the time."

"They might if it involved Lakeham being committed to an asylum on the same night," Guy said.

So off to the pub we went. I should point out that I seldom frequent such establishments so I did not know what to expect. Guy took Lily and me into the ladies lounge, which was a little shabby but nice enough.

"No children allowed in here," said the buxom woman behind the bar as she poured a pint for one of the locals.

"I can hardly leave her outside," I said.

"Let them be, Pearl," said the local, who sat in the bar on the other side. He was a thin man with a moustache. I remembered seeing him before. "I'll not say owt."

"Very well," said Pearl. "She can stay as long as she's quiet. The constable says."

"Oh, you're the constable," I said, smiling at the man. "I knew I'd seen you somewhere. We were staying at the

Abbey when there was that murder last year."

The constable looked from me to Guy then back again. "Didn't you have a different husband then?"

"I have the same husband now but he's busy in London," I told him firmly. "This is our cousin, Group Captain Marsh."

"Ah."

I got the feeling he didn't believe me, but it really didn't matter what he thought.

Guy ordered our drinks and came to sit with me. All the time, the landlady and the constable were watching us. I don't know what they expected us to do, in public and with my daughter sitting on my knee, but it was rather disconcerting.

"We're actually investigating," I explained, even though no explanation had been sought. Guy cast me a warning glance and I realised I should not have said it.

"Investigating?"

"Yes." In for a penny, I thought. "We're trying to find out about a fight that happened here about thirty years ago. I'm sure you were too young," I said to Pearl. "You too, Constable." I didn't really think that, but men do like to be complimented.

"Not that young," he said, taking a sip from his pint and smacking his lips. "But there's lots of fights in a place like this. Care to be more specific?"

"It was between John Lakeham and one of the locals."

"Ah, that fight," said the constable. I wished I could remember his name, but I did not want to ask him as it seemed rude to have forgotten. "Big Bert got what was coming to him if you ask me."

"That's what my dad always said," Pearl cut in. "Bert was asking for it."

"Big Bert?" Guy raised an eyebrow.

"His name is Bert Little, but folks around here call him Big Bert. He'd just got out of prison and was supposed to be keeping his nose clean. Then for some reason, he started on Mr Lakeham. More importantly, he

129

started on Mr Lakeham's wife, calling her all sorts, and her only a young lass. I know Bert was an idiot – we were at school together – but I don't know what got into him that night. Mr Lakeham wasn't hurting nobody."

I had to take a moment to work out the double negative. Country people talk so strangely at times.

"Where can we find Bert?" Guy asked.

"Where he usually is. The man's become institutionalised." Realising we did not understand him, the constable added. "In prison."

Bert Little

They knows me around these parts as Big Bert. Do you get it? Bert Little? Big Bert? Anyways, I remember when John Lakeham attacked me. Mad as a bloody hatter he was, like all the Lakehams. They've had murderers and thieves in that family for years, yet because they're rich and friends with the nobility, they gets away with it.

It was a Lakeham who put me into prison. John Lakeham's Aunty Matilda. She was a magistrate. She'd been one of those suffragettes too, and we all know what they're like. And what they don't like. Men. She made me suffer for that, she did. So what if I did steal old Ernie Harris's milk cart? It was a joke. Ernie's got no sense of humour. Never had one. Even when we was at school, he couldn't take a joke. Or a good beating. Seems to me that a boy should know what to do with his fists. Ernie'd just lie there, sobbing. The big girl's blouse! So I took his cart as a joke.

After I was found guilty, they brought up the other stuff I'd done, which meant I got a bigger sentence than I should have.

Anyways, where was I? Yeah, I'd just come out of prison and was in the pub, minding my own business, when John Lakeham comes in. I could see him looking at me, all funny like.

So I says to him, "Who do you think you're looking

at?"

Course he denies it. "I only want a peaceful drink," he says. "Please leave me alone."

He talked like a bloody pansy, if you ask me! God knows what that pretty little wife saw in him. So I says that to him. "Don't know what your pretty wife sees in you," I says. "She could have loads of men." Then for good measure I says, "From what I hear she has."

He lost his temper then, but didn't hit me. Just like Ernie bloody Harris. Well, I thought, if we're going to fight, he needs to throw the first punch, cos I ain't. Not when I've already been to prison. So I just says a few more things. I was only joking. Anyone could tell you.

Next thing you know, he's holding a broken bottle, and coming at me with it. That's not what I'd been expecting. I'd been told I mean, a man just doesn't do that. A man fights with his fists. Marquis of Queensbury rules.

Luckily, the doctor turns up and calms Lakeham down. I says, "Let's get the police," but the doctor gives me some money to keep it quiet. That's how the rich get away with everything. I don't mind though. It bought a round of drinks and the other fellas were saying how well I handled myself.

I thought I did good. Went above and beyond the call of duty, I did.

Percy Sullivan

I couldn't believe it when I saw my mother and Lily coming out of the local pub with Guy Marsh.

"Quick, Jennifer, go around the corner," I said.

She pulled my wheelchair backwards with a jerk and we hid until my mother and Guy had walked far enough the other way.

"What are they doing here?" I wondered aloud.

"Are they having an affair?" Jennifer asked.

"I don't know…" Even though I liked Guy a lot and thought him more exciting than my dull old father, the thought of him stealing my mother made me sad and not only because he was supposed to love Anne. "Oh God, I hope my parents don't get divorced as well. We'll both be underprivileged."

"At least we'll have each other," said Jennifer. "So we can stand up against everyone else."

"Yes, I suppose so. But I like my father. I thought Mother liked him too."

"The Group Captain is very handsome, though."

"Oh, shut up! You'll be running off with him next!"

"I wouldn't mind," Jennifer said. "Nor would Mummy. She says he's really dreamy. Like a film star."

"He's too old for you. He'll probably be dead soon." I don't know why I suddenly wished that on Guy.

"People don't die of old age when they're in their thirties."

"I shan't let my mother run away with him. I'll have a strong word with her about it. Better still, I'll tell my father. Anyway, he loves Anne. He's just forgotten that he does."

"Oh, don't, Percy! Because then if they split up, they'll blame you. It's best to let things be and hope they'll be happy again one day." Jennifer began to cry.

"Hey," I said, patting her hand. "Hey, there's no need to cry." I didn't know what to say or do. So I remembered something my father always said to my mother. "Things will look better in the morning."

"No, it won't, Percy. I love my mummy and daddy too, and I don't want them to divorce. Oh, I don't care about being underprivileged. I think that might even be rather character building for me. I should bear it quite well, I think. But I want them to stay together so we can be a family. I'm glad that awful Bunty woman is dead. She didn't care who she hurt. So why are we even bothering to find out the truth?"

"Because Anne is going to die and I don't want her to."

"Oh, yes, I'd forgotten about that." Jennifer sighed.

132

"When one has one's own problems, it's easy to forget what others are going through, but I must be a better person and think of Anne."

"I think you're quite a splendid person, Jennifer."

"Do you, Percy? I thought I upset you the other day when I said I'd bear your affliction much better than you."

"It was a rotten thing to say."

"I can't help it if it's the truth. I'm a woman and we're made of stronger stuff. That's why we have the babies. Men would never cope."

"I think I'd much rather spend nine months carrying a baby than the rest of my life in a wheelchair," I snapped.

"Yes, I hadn't thought of it that way. I suppose it must be rather grim. Sorry, Percy. Please, let's be friends again. If we're both going to be from broken homes, we have to stick together."

She had a point. I just wish she didn't always think she was so much better at everything. Men were supposed to be better than girls. All the boys at school said so and so did Father. Though I notice he never said it when Mother was around.

"We have to get our parents back together," I said, hoping to take control. "That'll be our secondary task, alongside clearing Anne's name."

"Oh, good idea, Percy! I think we should…"

"I haven't decided how we're going to do it yet. Let me think about it on the way to the Abbey."

"But what if…?"

"It's the secondary task, Jennifer," I reminded her. She would probably have a brilliant idea, and then I wouldn't be able to impress her with mine. I just hadn't thought of it yet.

We saw no one as Jennifer pushed me up the path towards the big front doors of the Abbey. There were a couple of steps to navigate, so she turned my wheelchair around and dragged it backwards, bumping up the steps one at a time. I bit back the pain. I could feel her puffy breath on my neck, which somehow made the pain more bearable.

"For someone so thin, you're really heavy," she said when she had pulled me to the top step.

"Sorry." I felt as though I had failed a test.

"It's not your fault. I'm just saying, that's all."

"Henry says it's because I'm a dead weight."

"That's not very nice," Jennifer huffed. "I do think you let him get away with too much sometimes."

"He's alright. I don't think he meant it in a horrible way. It's how nurses talk."

She knocked on the front door and it swung open, creaking loudly, like a door in a horror film.

"Someone must be here," she whispered. "Perhaps we should go…"

"No, just wheel me in and if anyone comes we'll say we were looking for Lily's dolly, just like you said. No one will suspect children of investigating."

"No, you're right."

She pushed me into the hallway, where we were met with our first obstacle. The stairs.

"Oh dear," said Jennifer. "I don't know if I can pull you and the wheelchair up there."

I almost wished we had brought Henry with us. He would have just carried me up and brought the wheelchair up afterwards. But Henry was relaxing back at Jennifer's house. He probably thought we were somewhere kissing. I must admit I was beginning to wish that was the case. Something about the empty house unnerved me. I felt as though it mocked me, with its stairs and locked doors. I wondered if a house could really send someone mad.

I didn't want Jennifer to know about my fears, so I sat up straight to show her just how unconcerned I was.

"We'd best search downstairs first," I suggested. "We might find some clues to the ghost."

"But there weren't any clues when we stayed here."

"Who knows? Perhaps the ghost came downstairs

when we had gone. Or perhaps now we know more, we'll know what clues to look for."

She agreed that was possible, so we began searching. We started in the drawing room, where the furniture was covered in dust sheets.

"The servants haven't been doing much," Jennifer said, running a finger along the mantelpiece in a way I had often seen my mother doing after our cleaner left for the day.

"They probably get fed up of looking after people," I said.

"If I were a servant I would be much better at my job," she insisted. "Even when there was no one to see my efforts."

"You always say things like that, Jennifer, but you don't really know."

"Things like what?" She frowned at me.

"That you'd be brilliant at things you don't actually have to do. How do you know until you try it?"

"Because I know." She sounded less sure, which made me feel bad.

"Of course, you would be brilliant," I agreed.

"There's no need to patronise me, Percy. It's not easy for girls. We're supposed to be dumb and let men do everything, so people don't like it if we say we'd be good at things. I don't want to be that sort of girl. I'm going to be good at everything, just to show people."

"I wasn't patronising you." With a sinking feeling, I realised that we were going to argue again. Sometimes I noticed that no matter what Father said to Mother, she took umbrage. One couldn't win where women were concerned. I wondered if love was supposed to be like this; always putting your foot in it. "Let's go to the room looking out onto to the terrace. The killer might have left something there."

"But Bunty Lemington-Smith was pushed from the roof."

"Where else can we look? We can't get upstairs. At

least we'd be doing something."

The terrace room was the library. All the furniture there had also been covered in dust sheets, and the wooden floor was caked with dirty footprints coming from the French windows.

"The servants have done a worse job in here," I said to Jennifer. "Someone has come in from the terrace after a storm, yet no one has cleaned it up."

"That's odd, Percy. Look at where the footprints go."

She pushed me over to the window, to the first set of footprints, and we followed their path. They stopped just before a wall next to the fireplace. In fact, one footprint appeared to be cut in half, with only the heel of the shoe showing.

"A secret passage!" Jennifer and I cried together.

"Just like in Enid Blyton," I said. I immediately regretted it. Surely she would think I was too old for those stories. "Not that I've read her books for a long time. I just remember."

"Yes, me too. But how do we open it?"

"There'll be a secret switch somewhere. I can't believe we were here the whole of last summer and didn't find this."

"A secret passage is supposed to stay hidden."

"Yes..." I fell silent.

"What's wrong?"

"You know when you have an inkling of something, but it just won't come to mind? A bit like having something on the tip of your tongue. Well, it's something like that. I've read something from all the people who have written to me about Anne and I think it's connected, but I can't remember what it is. It's so annoying."

"I'm sure I would be able to remember, if you had let me read the evidence. Women are better at remembering."

"Oh yes." I sighed. "I'm sure you would!"

"Oh, let's not argue again, Percy."

"Anyway, you can't read the evidence. I sent what I've got so far to Guy."

"Shall we find out how this door opens?" Jennifer asked.

"Yes, go on then. There's usually a switch or something on the fireplace."

It took us ages, touching every bit of carving and moving every ornament. Jennifer tried all the things I could not reach, but none of them opened up the door. I began to wonder if we'd imagined the footsteps leading into the wall.

"It's useless," I said. "We'll never find it."

"I wonder if it's behind the mirror," Jennifer said, pulling up the corner of the large mirror that covered the wall above the fireplace. We heard a sliding sound and the next thing we knew, a wooden panel next to the fireplace opened up, revealing a dark cavity.

"I found it!" Jennifer clapped her hands together.

"I would have found it if I could reach," I said.

"Yes, I know. We both found it, didn't we, Percy? By eliminating all other possibilities."

"Now who's patronising who?"

"Oh, honestly, if you're going to be like this…"

"No, you're right. I'm sorry. We both found it. Come on, let's go and explore."

My wheelchair only just fit through the gap in the wooden panel. "There's a torch in my bag, on the back of the chair," I told Jennifer. She got it out and handed it to me, so I could hold it whilst she pushed. The passageway went on for ages, and I think we went all the way from the East wing to the West wing, but as it twisted and turned, it was hard to work out where we ended up.

"But there's nothing," I said, when we reached the end. "Nothing at all. There should be stairs, leading up to the top floor. Or some sort of secret hidey hole where the priests used to go. Oh, hiding, that's it!"

"That's what?"

"When we were in the library did you notice a window seat?"

"I can't say I was looking."

"There isn't one."

"What has that to do with anything?"

"I don't know. I wish I could remember. But I'm sure someone mentioned there being one. Yet both windows are flush to the wall. There's no bay and not enough room behind the drapes for someone to hide."

"Let's turn around and head back," Jennifer suggested. "We can check again."

So we did that. I shone my torch everywhere, but could not find any other exit than the one to the terrace room. "It doesn't make sense," I said. The torch started to flicker, so I banged it against my hand, to try and get the batteries to go for longer. That never works, so I don't know why I even bothered.

We were halfway back towards the library when the torch died altogether. "Oh, bloody hell," I cried. Everything went black. Jennifer stopped pushing.

"Keep going," I said.

"I can't see where I'm going," she complained. "Percy, I'm afraid." She reached down for my hand.

I don't know why that made me feel glad. I suppose it was because Jennifer was always so sure of how brave and clever she was. It made a chap feel a bit inadequate. I squeezed her hand in the way I'd often seen Father do with Mother. "It will be alright. Just move slowly."

We moved forward a few yards. "We must be near the end," I said. "I can see some light around that corner." It reflected on the dark walls.

"I'm sure we haven't gone that far."

As quickly as it appeared, the light extinguished. "Someone is here," Jennifer whispered. "Oh Percy, why did we have to come snooping around?" We heard receding footsteps in the distance, similar to those I'd heard when Jennifer was on the floor above me the last time we explored the house. At least this time we were together. We waited to make sure they were going away from us, before moving on.

"The light was around that corner," I whispered back. "So keep going. We might be able to find out where it came from."

We carried on, and I think we both held our breath. When we turned the corner, there was something strange about the floor. "Wait," I said. "Stop a minute."

Jennifer did as I asked.

"Look, Jennifer. It's coming from down there."

On the floor was a long strip of pale light. "It's another door," she said, but she did not sound nearly as excited as she had before.

"Try to open it," I suggested.

"Okay." She did not sound very sure. "What if it's the real murderer, Percy?"

"There are two of us and no one can kill two people at once. I'll distract them while you run for help." I wasn't entirely sure what I said was correct, but I made it sound as if it would be.

"Percy…"

"Go on, it will be alright."

She squeezed past my wheelchair and I think she put her hand against the wall. All I could really see was the strip of light illuminating her feet. Suddenly the light grew wider.

"Oof," Jennifer went as she suddenly fell forward. I tried to catch her, but was too far away. She only just managed to right herself.

"Percy!" she said, standing wide eyed near the doorway. I rolled forward and looked in. It was a chamber, lit only with a gaslight. On the walls were dozens of playbills and film posters, all showing the same woman. There was a dressing table, with three mirrors, and an open trunk full of sparkling clothes.

Standing next to a four poster bed, draped with red velvet curtains, was a woman dressed in white chiffon.

"Hello, children," the ghost of Lakeham Abbey said.

Chapter Nine

Celia Sullivan

I must admit I found it difficult to understand the direction in which Guy's investigations took us. We were supposed to be finding out how Anne murdered his father and Bunty, yet he seemed more interested in Eleanor Grace's early life.

She had been brought up in the vicinity of Lakeham Abbey, and had once worked in the kitchens of a big hotel somewhere on the London road.

"That was where she met John Lakeham," Guy told me, as we drove there. I was still reeling after seeing Percy and Jennifer across the road. Luckily they disappeared around the corner and I don't think they noticed us, but having told my son to stay away from the Abbey, I could hardly explain why I was there.

"What's the point of all this, Guy?" I asked. "Do you think Eleanor Grace killed your father? Is that it?"

"It's possible."

"But if Eleanor Grace committed suicide, she could not have killed Bunty."

"If she committed suicide," Guy said. "Her body was never found, remember?"

"And you think Anne is covering for her?"

"That is also possible."

"Even as far as being executed in her place?"

"I believe Anne is that loyal to those she loves, yes."

"If what you say is true, Guy, she won't thank you for exposing her mother."

"I don't care, Celia. Don't you see? Whether it was Eleanor or Anne who killed my father, if we find Eleanor in hiding, then we can create reasonable doubt. They have to look at Anne's case. There are just a few days to go to her execution. I have to put a stop to it."

"What if she did kill your father?"

"I have to believe that she didn't."

"You'd never know," I said. "Not for certain. Even if they let her out. If she's mad, like her father, you'd never be sure she wouldn't put a knife in you one night whilst you were asleep."

"It's a risk I'm willing to take. The other day I read up about Edith Thompson's execution. It was awful and painful and bloody. No woman should die like that. No matter what she's done."

His eyes were dark pools of misery. I had known he had a thing for Anne, but I hadn't realised it was something like an obsession. Like Bunty's obsession, a small voice said. I shivered, cuddling Lily closer to me. Her warm little cheek soothed my soul.

"No matter what we find or don't find, I'm going home tomorrow, Guy," I told him. "I need to be with Freddie."

"I understand. Thank you for coming. I know you probably don't believe in Anne as I do but—"

"Strangely, I do. I remember how she went out of her way to make us all happy, and I know I can be silly and very wrong about people." Bunty for a start, I thought, but did not say. "But I can't believe it was all an act. I really do believe she wanted to create a happy family situation for us all. Perhaps because her family was not happy. I'd even go so far as to believe she might have killed Bunty because Bunty was the only fly in the ointment, so to speak. She brought bitterness and envy with her wherever she went. But don't you see, Guy, that if Anne didn't kill Bunty, it means someone else in the house did. Perhaps even a member of our family. None of us would ever be completely sure of each other."

The hotel was in an old Georgian manor, with extensive grounds. I supposed that, like my parents, the owners had to sell it because of their taxes, and so for the last forty years or more it had been a country hotel. I blushed to realise it was the sort of place where men brought their secretaries and was glad Percy had not seen me and Guy here or he might get the wrong idea entirely. It was still nicer than the cheap hotel in which we had been staying.

The reception desk was deserted, so Guy banged on the bell. A flustered young woman came out of the office, saying, "Yes, Mr Granger. I'll see to it that gets done."

I wanted to suggest that she tidy up her lipstick, and put a comb through her hair, as her conference with Mr Granger seemed to have dishevelled both, but I left the talking to Guy.

"Hello there," he said, in his most charming voice. The girl visibly relaxed and I think she totally forgot about Mr Granger and her smudged lipstick. "I am looking for someone who might have worked in this hotel thirty or forty years ago."

"What do you want to know that for?" the girl asked, her eyes narrowing suspiciously.

"I'm a reporter and I'm investigating the disappearance of Eleanor Grace for a newspaper article."

"Oh…we get lots of her fans here asking about her. I wasn't born then, but she used to work in the kitchens."

"Yes, that's what we heard. Is there anyone who remembers that time?"

"Yes, Connie in the kitchen. She was a kitchen maid back then. She worked with Miss Grace – she was Pargeter in those days – and Maudie."

"Oh yes, we know Maudie," I said. The girl barely noticed I was there. She only had eyes for Guy. "She cooks for my family now." I could barely afford her, but Percy had been adamant that we should help her.

"Could we speak to Connie?" Guy asked.

"I'll see if she can come up. It's nearly lunch time, so they'll be busy."

I was expecting an elderly woman, but Connie was only in her late forties or early fifties.

"I was only twelve when I started working here," she told us as we took tea in the lounge. "Helen – Eleanor – and Maudie were a couple of years older. Maudie worked in the kitchen and Helen was a chambermaid."

"Did you ever meet John Lakeham?" Guy asked.

"Oh yes. He was very handsome. He used to stay here when he'd been drinking in the bar, rather than drive back to the Abbey. He met Helen on her night off. She used to dress up and go in to the bar. The management didn't like it, but she was a good actress even then. She could pretend to be older, and with a wig, looked like a completely different person so even the managers didn't recognise her. Not that she fooled Mr Lakeham in any deceitful way. He knew exactly who and what she was, but he loved her anyway. She was the sort of girl who inspired love in men. Sometimes to bad effect."

"What do you mean by that?" I asked.

"Well, some men got silly over her. She used to laugh and say she couldn't help it. But there was one man who hung around a lot. I didn't like him. He'd got a bad reputation."

"With women?" I suggested.

"Oh no. With drugs."

"What was he? Some sort of dealer?" Guy asked.

"No." She shook her head then seemed to change her mind. "Well, yes. I suppose you'd call it that. But he had legal access to drugs, so he never got caught. I'm surprised he hasn't been reported, but when someone is respected as a professional…well… There's some as never get in trouble, isn't there?"

Guy and I exchanged glances.

"Do you remember his name?" asked Guy.

"He was one of the Lakehams," Connie said. "Distant cousin, or something. So he had a different name."

When she told us the name, I was shocked, and thought that Connie must have got it wrong. We thanked her and made our way to the foyer.

"It's rubbish," I said. "Sheer nonsense." (I do hope Percy appreciates how much thought I have given to dramatic tension here in not naming the person!)

"Is it?" Guy looked at me and I felt a bit silly again, as if I had not quite caught up. "Is it really? I've been reading Percy's papers, and I had a feeling that something was not quite right."

"Guy…" I put my hand on his arm. "He's a respected—"

"Celia!" A voice rang out across the foyer. I turned to see Freddie standing near to the reception desk.

"Darling, what are you doing here?" I ran to him, but his face told me that he was in no mood to give me a kiss.

"I might ask you the same thing."

"We're investigating."

"Is that what they're calling it nowadays? I should call you out, Marsh."

"Freddie," Guy said, putting up his hands. "Nothing is going on, I swear. Celia has just been giving me moral support."

"I'm sure she has. Anyway, Celia, I don't know why you're here, but I'm here for our son. I received a telephone call from Percy earlier today asking me to meet him at the Abbey tonight. I just came here to book a room first. He said if I found you, I was to bring you along. He knows you're here. Honestly, I can't believe you let him see you with your lover!"

"Freddie…"

"We'll talk about it later. We had better go and see what our son wants."

Anne Pargeter

It's difficult to explain prison life to those who have no experience of it. Holloway is a grim building, as befits a place where people are sent to be punished. Every now and then charitable groups come in and make recommendations, but those suggestions are never carried through. The public believe we deserve to be treated like animals so resent any taxes spent on making our lives easier. I suppose we are animals to them. So we sleep in hard, lice-ridden beds and eat food that pigs would turn their snouts up at.

For someone awaiting execution, the days are interminable. Edith Thompson, who was the last woman to be executed in nineteen twenty-three, suffered dreadfully from nerves and had to be carried to the scaffold. I am more resigned than that, because I have made the choice to be here, yet I fear that my courage will desert me at the last minute and I will disgrace myself. Or the whole thing could go terribly wrong…

I overhear the other inmates talking with great relish about the way Edith Thompson died, mainly because it's not going to happen to them. Her execution went horribly wrong, leading to a haemorrhage that suggested she might have been with child when they hanged her. That has been refuted, but I wonder if the authorities did so because they were afraid to admit they had got it wrong. I do know that one of the executioners was so disturbed by events, he immediately resigned. This was a man who spent his life executing prisoners and had probably seen the worst of it all.

My own execution is imminent and with that in mind they have already begun to give me sedatives. I even look forward to them every morning, counting the minutes until I can put the tablet on my tongue and float away to oblivion for a few hours. It helps me to understand how she has become reliant to the point that she is afraid to leave her hiding place and return to the world. Will my death shock her out of her reverie? Does she even know I am here? If she does, has she simply left me to rot? Yet this is what I want, so why should she try to save me?

When one is so completely alone, and facing her last days, it is easy to think the worst even of those we love.

Oh, Hotspur, my young friend, I am so sorry to wallow in self-pity like this. I know that you are fighting for me, and I want to be brave for your sake, but I am very afraid of this course I have taken.

Sometime later…

I am writing this quickly as I do not know if I will get a chance to finish it. As I was writing earlier, one of the screws came and said, "Mr Marsh is here to see you."

My heart flipped. Guy? Did he want more answers or had he come to add to my torment by telling me exactly what he thought of the woman he believed had killed his father?

I was taken to a small interview room and waited as they let him in. I held my breath when the door opened. But it was not Guy. It was his brother, Andrew.

"Miss Lakeham," he said, nodding curtly. Detective Marsh sat down opposite me. "I wish to ask you a question."

"I have already told you that I have nothing to say, Mr Marsh. And as I am to be executed, you have very little to hold over me."

"Where are the keys?"

I was taken aback. It was the last thing I was expecting to be asked. "Keys?"

"To the upper floors at Lakeham Abbey. You are the legal owner of Lakeham Abbey, are you not?"

"That is correct."

"So you must know where the keys are."

I shook my head. "I don't. I've never had them. I assumed they were lost many years ago." That was not strictly true, but I was not going to be too honest with him.

"So you have never had access to the upper rooms?"

"No… At least…I found one of the doors open one day and went upstairs. Percy Sullivan's camera and walkie talkies were up there, so I assumed the children had somehow managed to find a way to open the door. But when I went back to look the door was locked again.

I really don't have the keys."

"I believe you," he said. "Now your warder is going to take you back so you can change out of your prison clothes into something more suitable and you're going to come with me."

"Where?"

"To find out the truth once and for all."

I did not like the sound of that. "You mean I can leave the prison? But…" Strange as it seemed, after spending nearly a year incarcerated I had become used to the security of Holloway's walls and feared leaving them.

"I have the permission of the Home Secretary to take you back to Lakeham Abbey. Hurry along, Miss Lakeham. We do not have long."

"Will I be coming back here?"

"That remains to be seen."

So I am to leave Holloway. As I head into the unknown, I wonder about you, Hotspur. I wonder where you are and I hope that you and Lily are safe and that you always will be.

Percy Sullivan

I asked Henry to take me up to the roof, with Jennifer coming up behind us, carrying my wheelchair.

When we got there and I was safely back in my chair, I saw that he had set the chairs out in a circle, just as I asked. Only one part of the circle was not closed and it was into this that I was wheeled.

I looked around at everyone and for a moment felt shy. After all I was just a stupid boy in a wheelchair. Yet Guy had told me it was my show.

"You can do it, Percy," he said, nodding. "None of us would be here without your passion and drive." He looked across at Anne. It made me sad to see her. She had lost a lot of weight and was very pale. Prison pallor, I think they call it. She glanced at Guy under her lashes. I had hoped they would be sitting close together, but she was on the far side, with his stepbrother and a prison

147

warder sitting either side of her.

"Does Anne have to wear handcuffs?" I asked.

"She does for now," said Detective Marsh.

Anne smiled at me sadly. "I'm alright, Hotspur. At least, I'll have some fresh air before…" She fell silent. "I wonder what this is all about," she added. I could see she was trying to be cheerful. "It seems you've been awfully busy for my sake."

"This is very irregular," said Mr Carstairs. "What is going on, Jennifer?" His wife sat next to him, chewing her bottom lip.

"Percy will explain, Daddy," she said. "He's been awfully clever, putting it all together."

"Percy, darling?" asked my mother, "What have you been up to?" She didn't sound angry with me. Just afraid. My father sat next to her, and she had Lily on her knee, but my sister was struggling to get off. Mother let her down onto the floor, but held onto her hand. I sensed that Mother and Father were not very happy to be together and it made me feel sad. What if I had brought about their divorce? I might even have pushed Mother into Guy's arms. I tried not to think about it too much.

"I've been investigating, Mother. You know I have."

"Good show," said Doctor Aitken, who sat next to my mother. "The lad is playing Sherlock Holmes." He grinned. "It'll be interesting to see what he's come up with." He looked at his watch. "I hope you won't be too long, dear boy. I do have patients to see."

"Go on, Percy," said Guy. "Tell us what it's all about."

"Well, you helped me, really," I said, still a bit unsure of myself. "You know, telling me the bits of the puzzle that you and Mother filled in."

"But all this is happening because you believed, Percy," said Guy.

"It would be nice," said Mrs Carstairs, "if we could get on with just what Percy believed. I must say, Celia, I'm not at all happy that he's dragged Jennifer all over

148

Lakeham Abbey chasing goodness knows what theories."

"I wanted to come, Mummy," said Jennifer. "Please, just let Percy tell you what he knows."

"Very well," I said, trying to sound a bit more grown up. I pushed my wheelchair into the centre, and Henry, as I had asked him, moved to fill the space I left open. "It started for us with the murder of Bunty Lemington-Smith. This is a story of an obsession that goes back many years."

"Oh, good show," said Doctor Aitken, clapping. "Sounds like a corker, lad."

"I'll start with the Carstairs and Mr Carstairs's obsession with who Jennifer's real father is." Luckily, I had explained it all to Jennifer so she wouldn't cry or anything – again.

"Steady on," said Mr Carstairs. Mrs Carstairs just choked slightly.

"Bunty Lemington-Smith hinted that Mrs Carstairs had not been honest about the baby she was carrying when she married. Jennifer was premature, which suggested that Mrs Carstairs was already carrying her when they married. This doubt led Mr Carstairs into the arms of another woman – his secretary – but it also gave both him and his wife a reason to murder Bunty."

"I said steady on!" Mr Carstairs stood up. "Do I really have to listen to this? I'm a busy man." He moved towards the edge of the circle.

"Sit down," said Guy. "Let him finish." Guy's brother stood up too, blocking Mr Carstairs's way so he had no choice but to go back to his seat.

"If the truth about any of it came out," I went on, "then Mr Carstairs's career in parliament would be over, not to mention the scandal of his own affair. So Mr Carstairs had both the motive and the opportunity of killing Bunty. As did Mrs Carstairs."

"But we did not," said Mr Carstairs. "I may not be a perfect man but I am no killer!"

149

"No, I know," I said. "You didn't kill Bunty and neither did your wife. Also, Jennifer is yours, Mr Carstairs. You only have to look at her to see that."

"Of course she's yours," said Mrs Carstairs, her eyes filling with tears. "Angus, whatever mistakes I made before we married, I never deceived you. Jennifer was born early. You know that, Angus. You know damn well we nearly lost her."

"I've been such a fool," Mr Carstairs said, lowering his head. "How could I ever doubt?"

"Oh, Daddy," Jennifer said, bursting into tears. She ran to her father and sat on his knee. At the same time he and his wife held hands. If I had done nothing else good, I think I managed to stop them from getting divorced. No matter how much Jennifer thought she could manage with being underprivileged, I didn't think she really could. But now I had to deal with my own parents.

"The other obsession," I said, when things had quietened down, "was my father's obsession with not having fought in the war."

"Percy," said my mother. "You're surely not going to give your father a reason to have murdered Bunty, are you?"

"I am afraid so, Mother. So please, be quiet and let me get on with it. Earlier today I spoke to a Mr Cohen, who lives in Golders Green. He told me that for the past couple of years my father has been helping smugglers to bring certain items out of Eastern Europe. The transportation of antiquities is a perfect way of getting contraband into the country. And if Father was found out, it could mean prison. That was a pretty solid reason for killing Bunty."

"Percy," my father huffed.

"Only my father wasn't smuggling contraband at all, were you, Father?"

"No, but I'm very angry with Mr Cohen for telling you the truth." Even as he said it, I don't think he really meant it.

"Mr Cohen, and lots of men and families just like him, lost everything they had when they fled Europe," I told everyone. "The Nazis took it all, even down to the gold fillings in teeth. We've all seen the *Pathe* newsreels of the camps, I'm sure. Father has been helping Jewish families to get some of their belongings back, using his department at the university as a cover. He might be in trouble if it came out, especially with the Soviet Embassy, but I don't think anyone would want to put him in prison. It was a really brave thing to do, Father."

"I hardly did anything," my father said, coughing a little.

"I think it was brave," said my mother. "Freddie, you're wonderful."

The way my father was looking at my mother, I don't think he was in the mood for her compliments.

"Now," I said, "we come to my mother, and an obsession that has led to misery not just for others but for me."

"Oh, Percy, please don't, darling," my mother entreated (implored, pleaded).

She let go of Lily without realising and my sister began toddling around the circle. First she went to Anne, who stroked her head, despite wearing handcuffs. "Hello, darling girl," Anne whispered.

"When I read about your friendship with Bunty from when you were at school, Mother, I realised straight away that Bunty was obsessed with you from the moment she met you. She undermined you all the time, and tried to stop you from finding someone to love. That was why you married Father in such a hurry. You knew Bunty was in hospital and couldn't try to stop you as she had before. Guy found out that Bunty was really in an asylum, put there by her awful aunt. But just because Bunty's aunt was awful doesn't mean Bunty was a victim. The truth is that she was a dreadful woman who gave you a very good reason for killing her, Mother."

"Percy…" My mother's voice sounded hoarse.

"Please don't… I couldn't bear it if you knew."

"I do know, Mother. I think I remember, but even if I didn't remember, it makes sense. She wanted you to be as unhappy as she was, so she tried to hurt those you loved. It was Bunty who let me fall down the stairs when I was a baby. No, she didn't just let me fall. She pushed me. Didn't she?"

"I didn't want to believe it," Mother said, looking around the circle with wide, stricken eyes. "She was supposed to be my best friend. And the idea of anyone hurting a child – my child – it was unthinkable. I thought it must be my fault, because I'd been so tired that day and I hadn't been the mother I always wished I could be. It couldn't possibly have been Bunty. Only deep down I knew it was. I never forgave myself, Percy." Mother turned to my father. "I know you think I'm having an affair with Guy, but I'm not. Everything I've done over the past few days, and the reason I've been pushing everyone to help, has been about making up for what happened to Percy. He loves Anne, and he doesn't want her to die, so I want to stop that from happening if I can. I just want to help my boy to be happy. But it's you I love, Freddie. I always have, always will."

"Even though you married me to escape Bunty," Father said.

"Oh, you silly goose. I married you because I was afraid that if I didn't, someone else would snap you up. And yes, if it was also to stop Bunty from spoiling things, then that too. Because I wasn't going to lose you, Freddie, not to anyone or for anyone."

"Darling Celia…"

Then something awful happened. My mother and father kissed. In front of everyone. I've never been so embarrassed in my life.

"So," I said, loudly, bringing a halt to their silliness. "You did have a motive for killing Bunty, Mother."

"Oh yes, I suppose so and I can't say I'm sorry she's dead. But I didn't kill her."

"I know you didn't, Mother. You and Father were together all that night. Kissing, I suppose." I rolled my eyes.

"Something like that," my father agreed. I didn't ask what the something like kissing was.

"But," I continued, "this story is partly about Bunty's obsession with finding things out about people. She tried to find out about Anne, but she also tried to find out about Lakeham Abbey. On the night she died, she went exploring. She found, as Jennifer and I did, the secret passageway off the library."

"A secret passageway?" Mrs Carstairs looked excited. "I'd heard these old houses had them, but I didn't know the Abbey did. How exciting. What did she find?"

"Murder," I said, gravely. I ignored Guy's grin. "But also a playbill with Eleanor Grace's name on it. She had it in her hand when she died. She had found her way up to this very roof and the murderer was here, smoking a cigarette. That's when she was pushed off the roof."

"Well, yes, we know that," said Mr Carstairs. "It was Miss Pargeter. Lakeham. Whatever her name is. And may I say that I'm surprised she has been let out of prison. Isn't her execution tomorrow?"

"Oh, Daddy!" Jennifer cried. She had been sitting on his knee, but she moved back to her chair in a huff. "Don't you know that all this has been about clearing Anne's name?"

"We have special dispensation from the Home Secretary," Detective Marsh said. "Miss Lakeham is permitted to be here in order to help us complete our enquiries."

"The real story of obsession goes back much further," I said, feeling that we were getting off the point a bit. "Erm… Guy?" To be honest I had run out of words and steam. I had not realised how exhausting it was for detectives to tick off suspects one by one. My mouth was dry. "Perhaps you could pick this up."

"Thank you, Percy." Guy stood up, and I moved back

153

to my space in the circle. "As Percy said, this story has been about obsession all along. But not Bunty's obsession with finding out the worst of everyone, though that did bring about her death. There is something insidious about this house. Do you feel it?" He looked at Anne when he spoke.

"Yes," she said, quietly. "Yes, I feel it. I've always felt it, despite my best efforts to turn it into a happy place."

"It drives people to madness and has done so for years. Previous owners have committed terrible crimes in order to keep it in the family. Our story really begins about thirty-one years ago, before Anne was born. John Lakeham was a known drug addict who fell in love with a beautiful young girl. The story of their marriage and his descent into madness is well known. What is not known is that John Lakeham got his drugs from a family member; a distant cousin who had access to the best heroin that money could buy. What John did not know was that the cousin had his eye on Lakeham Abbey." Guy paused for effect, letting everyone take in his words. "If John were to die, the Abbey would naturally go to the cousin. Then Helen Pargeter – later to become the actress, Eleanor Grace – entered the picture and the cousin's obsession shifted. He not only wanted the house. He wanted the girl and the house. The cousin hit a snag. When John fell in love, he decided to clean up his act. He refused to take heroin anymore. This led to some difficult times for young Helen. She was hardly equipped to deal with a man withdrawing from drugs. Thinking she could trust the cousin, and not knowing about his obsession or his role in supplying drugs to her husband, she turned to him for help. He gave John medication that was supposed to help him, but in fact only kept him in the grip of his addiction, finally leading to a breakdown in the local pub and incarceration in a mental home, where John Lakeham apparently took his own life."

No one spoke when Guy stopped speaking. We were

all too interested in what he had to say. I knew it all and even I was enthralled.

"But he didn't take his own life," I said, wanting to be part of the drama. "He was murdered."

"That's right, Hotspur," said Guy. "He was murdered."

"Well, sort of," I said.

"How?" asked Anne. She looked paler than ever.

"It could not have been you as you had not yet been born," Guy said in a soft voice. "We found out that someone visited John at the asylum only the day before he died. We believe, though we don't have proof, that they slipped John a razor blade and made a recommendation that John do the 'honourable' thing for his wife and child and kill himself. Soon after, Helen moved away, taking a new name and a new life in the theatre. No one thought anything of it at the time."

"And how do you know what Helen did?" asked Doctor Aitken. Guy winked at me, just as we had arranged.

"I'm glad you asked us that, Doctor. Henry?" It was the moment I had been waiting for.

Henry went over to the attic door and opened it. A woman dressed all in white came out onto the roof.

"Please, everyone, say hello to the ghost of Lakeham Abbey," I said.

"Mother…" Anne stood up and I noticed that the policeman and the warder didn't stop her when she ran into Eleanor's arms, hampered somewhat by the handcuffs.

"Oh, my darling, Mary-Ann, I'm so sorry," Eleanor said, stroking Anne's hair. "I didn't know. I swear I didn't know. I would have come forward."

"No, you mustn't," Anne sobbed. "You mustn't. It's all finished with, Mother. You can live free now."

"How can I ever be free when my little girl is suffering?"

"So she wasn't dead at all?" said my mother. "Did

Eleanor Grace kill Bunty to keep her secret?"

"Mary-Ann thought I did, didn't you, darling?" asked Eleanor. "Just as she thought I had killed George Peterson and I believed she had done it. If only we had spoken to each other, but things were so chaotic at the time and I was being controlled by..." She stopped. "Well, that's for later in the story, isn't it, young Percy?"

"Henry, get Miss Grace a chair, please," I said. I was dying to look around and see the reaction to her appearance, but Guy had warned me to play it cool. "So we can finish telling the story."

"This is a turn up for the books," said Doctor Aitken. He was the only one who didn't sit back down.

"Yes, it is, isn't it, Stanley?" Eleanor Grace looked at him sharply.

"What happened after you left the Abbey?" Detective Marsh asked her. "When your husband died, I mean."

"The Lakeham family chased me off. They said that the marriage was never really legal and I had no claim on anything. Remember, I was only sixteen years old and expecting a baby. I was not a stupid girl, but I had no idea of the law. So I believed them. It was George Peterson who put me on the right track. He was my solicitor – before we became friends – and he explained that my daughter was the rightful owner of the Abbey. So when Mary-Ann was old enough, and I had enough money to support us both, we came to claim it back. Do you remember, Mary-Ann?"

"Yes, I remember."

"Strange things started to happen. I became confused and anxious. That was when George and Mary-Ann called in Doctor Aitken. Things did not improve. I became more upset, especially as Mary-Ann had not taken to George. He was a good man, Mr Marsh," Eleanor said to Guy. "A troubled man, but still a good man. I want you to know that. It seems to be my lot in life to fall in love with such men..." Her eyes became sad. "Perhaps that is why Mary-Ann was unsure about him. He was not the first 'bad boy' I loved after my husband... When George died, I thought she had done it, but I didn't come by that idea all on my own, did I, Stanley?"

Doctor Aitken shrugged. "I'm not sure what you mean, Eleanor. You had lots of strange fancies at the time. It was hard to keep up with them."

"You made sure of that. Just as you made sure that my husband stayed a drug addict and died in an asylum and how you've made sure that I am addicted to the medicines you've given me for the past fifteen years."

"I'm not sure I follow," said Mrs Carstairs. "I thought that was John Lakeham's cousin."

"What better person to have access to different drugs than a doctor?" Guy said. "Doctor Aitken is John Lakeham's cousin, Mrs Carstairs. He has been identified by one of the staff at the hotel where Helen worked. And by Helen herself, of course. Andrew also has the testimony of a man called Bert Little, who was put up to fighting John Lakeham by Doctor Aitken."

"I didn't know he was supplying John, I truly didn't," said Eleanor. "But I felt something was wrong, which was why I didn't take much persuading to move away and change my name. As I said, I was only sixteen and unsure of myself. So when Mary-Ann and George suggested we call Stanley Aitken in to help me with my anxiety, I put my doubts aside. After all, he had always seemed kind enough. Then, when George died, Stanley was there to help me to hide so that people would think I had done it. He convinced me that Mary-Ann had the same madness as her father, but I could not bear the thought of her being taken to an asylum.

"So we faked my death, but I never truly left Lakeham Abbey. Stanley knew about the secret passageway and a chamber in which I could hide. I did it so that Mary-Ann could be free," she said, putting her hand over her daughter's. "But I didn't realise how much I had been manipulated or how much I would come to rely on Stanley. Or at least on the drugs he gave me."

"So you killed Bunty," said Doctor Aitken. "Because she found you on this roof and you couldn't let her tell anyone else."

"Yes, she did find me, or at least evidence of me, but I didn't kill her, Stanley. You know that."

"You did it," I said. "You killed her, Doctor Aitken. Just like you made sure your cousin died in the asylum by slipping him a razor blade. And you killed Guy's father, George Peterson, because you saw him as a rival for Eleanor's affections."

"But you convinced me that Mary-Ann had done it, and let her think that I had done it," said Eleanor. "All these years I've wasted, unable to see my daughter, because I thought I was keeping her safe, when really you've been keeping me a prisoner."

"How ridiculous!" the doctor said. "Are you all going to believe the word of a neurotic woman who has been hiding from the police for years?"

"No, we'll believe the evidence," said Detective Marsh. "We know from the visitor book that you visited John Lakeham at the asylum just before he died. We also know that you've been offering your patients little extras over the years. You have quite a lucrative drug business going there, Doctor Aitken. Your outgoings far exceed your legal income. We also have all the empty bottles of pills that you've been feeding Miss Grace for years. Our scientists will check them, but I will hazard a guess that they don't hold the mild sedatives listed on the front of the bottle."

"It's all bloody ridiculous." Doctor Aitken became agitated. "Taking an innocent man and blaming him for the crimes of two mad women! They were in on it together. They killed George Peterson together and then they killed Bunty Lemington-Smith. Together! Why else would she hide? Why else would her daughter admit to killing Bunty?"

"I did it so my mother could be free," Anne explained.

"I guessed she was hiding here when some of her fans wrote to me saying they had seen her in the grounds. I came here last year to find her. I admit that I thought she might have killed George and Bunty, but that she had done so to protect me. I believed that if I admitted both murders, she would be free at last. I would have done anything so she could come out of hiding."

"I didn't know you'd been arrested," said Eleanor. "I have been so cut off from the world. I have only seen what Stanley wanted me to see. Sometimes I manage to get out. I saw you sleeping in your bed, Mary-Ann. I could hardly believe it... But he convinced me I had imagined it. But I kept on seeing you... Only my medication... I was confused."

"You're mad, that's what you are!" Doctor Aitken raged. "Mad." His eyes bulged in his head and I think we could all see where the real madness lay. Everyone stood up again.

Suddenly, he snatched up Lily, who was sitting on the ground near to his feet, and went over to the parapet with her. My mother screamed and my father swore. "Come any closer and I'll drop her."

"Put the child down, Doctor Aitken," said Detective Marsh.

I had not thought much of my sister. I mean, she was there and I supposed I was fond of her. We always liked listening to the Ovaltineys together. But I began to realise that I actually loved her quite a lot. She started to bawl and I had a sick and helpless feeling in my tummy.

"Oh, Lily," my mother cried. "Don't you hurt her, you brute!" She started to run forward but the doctor shook Lily and caused my mother to stop in her tracks.

"Put her down, Stanley," said Eleanor Grace. "She's just a child. She has done nothing to hurt you."

"What would you know?" he asked. "You never cared about me. After all the things I did for you."

"What did you do for me, Stanley?"

"We could have been happy in this house. If you

hadn't insisted on loving John instead of me. Oh, and then I had to stand by and watch whilst you paraded your lovers in front of me, onscreen and off. Why did you always love every other man but me? And her. Mary-bloody-Ann. Why was she more important to you than me?"

"She's my child, just as that little girl is Mr and Mrs Sullivan's child. You wouldn't hurt a child, would you, Stanley?"

"Wouldn't I? Don't you know how hard I tried to make you miscarry that brat? I thought that John's death would do it, but no, you clung on to her. Well, I wasn't going to have George Peterson taking you from me as well. I knew that if he was out of the picture, along with Mary-Ann, you'd see that I was the right man for you."

"And you are, Stanley. I'm just sorry I never told you. Now, please, put the child down safely and we'll discuss it."

"You don't mean it, Helen. You'll never mean it. Now back off, everyone, or I'll drop this child, so help me God. Do you think she'll make as much noise as Bunty made falling?" He laughed in a way that could only be described as maniacal, like the villain in a film. It felt like we were watching a film too, because in real life people don't do things like that to innocent little girls.

"Oh, dear God," my mother said. She fell against my father. "Lily, baby…"

I knew I had to do something but I didn't know what. I was in a wheelchair and people in wheelchairs are pretty useless most of the time. Or at least that's what everyone thought. Perhaps, I wondered, I could use that misconception (fallacy, delusion) to fool Doctor Aitken.

I tried to catch Anne's eye, but she was moving slowly. I noticed she was positioning herself behind Doctor Aitken. Finally she looked at me and I looked at her and we both nodded together.

"I'm the one you really want to punish, aren't I?" she said to the doctor.

He spun around to face her, so that he had his back to me. It also meant that Lily wasn't as far over the parapet as she had been. I would have to be very careful to make sure he didn't drop her. What if I got it wrong? Would it be my fault if Lily died? I felt nauseous and so afraid of doing the wrong thing, but I could see no other way out.

"Let her go and punish me instead," said Anne.

"That's a very tempting offer."

There was no more time to think. I lurched forward in my wheelchair, driving the wheels into the backs of the doctor's legs, so that he buckled and almost ended up in my lap. As he did so, Anne snatched Lily and quickly handed her to my mother.

"Oh, thank God," Mother said, hugging Lily and kissing her over and over again.

"Good boy, Hotspur," said Anne.

The doctor clambered up, which I was glad of as he was quite heavy on my legs. I saw the policeman come forward with some handcuffs, but he was too late. The doctor screamed "You!"

In the confusion, he made a grab for Anne and dragged her over the parapet with him.

Chapter Ten

Guy Marsh

It was winter when I returned to Lakeham Abbey. The trees were bare and the house, in the bleak December air, looked more haunted than ever. A chill wind crossed the marshes, biting through my flannel trousers.

Many months had passed since I was last here. At first, I had to go and see my mother, to tell her the truth about my father's death. They say that the truth will set you free, but I do not think it has brought either of us any peace to know that my father was no more than an innocent bystander in a drama that began long before he met Eleanor Grace. I have not had the heart to tell Eleanor Grace that my father was disbarred – for being drunk during an important trial – a few years before he met her. Neither have I the heart to tell her that I believe my father followed the money. He never really had enough for the playboy life he liked to live so attaching himself to the mother of a young heiress would ensure he lived the high life for a little longer.

Perhaps I am being unfair. Perhaps he did change. I will never know because I cannot ask him. It is hard to square the 'good' man that Eleanor insisted he was with the errant husband and father who abandoned us both. Perhaps we are not all just one thing, but are made of many different parts; some good, some bad.

My father is another reason I have stayed away. I do not want to follow the money. So I have been working hard, building up my business. I now own two planes, and whilst I am not rich, I am making a good living.

I went up to the house and asked after Anne. I feared that I had left things too late. I was not there for her when she

162

faced death in the prison and I had not been there as she recovered from her injuries after Doctor Aitken pulled her over the parapet.

They told me that she was over on the island. "She goes there a lot," Maudie said. It was the most I had ever heard the woman say. I guessed from her more refined clothes that she had become Eleanor's companion. I did not see Eleanor.

"She doesn't come out much," Maudie explained. "It's hard for her, after all those years in solitude. But she's getting better every day. Especially now she has Anne to help her."

I rowed over to the island, noticing that there were a couple of boats on the other bank. I saw Henry sitting amongst the shrubs smoking a cigarette, so I guessed that Percy was not far off.

I found him with Anne and Jennifer, sitting in our clearing. Odd how I thought of it in those terms. It was where we had the picnic and where Percy first said he saw the ghost. I had not really believed him, but it was now clear that he had seen Eleanor as she took a walk through the upper floors of the house.

Whereas before they had worn summer clothes, they were all wrapped up in thick coats and scarves. Yet, there was still the remains of a picnic on the ground, only this time they appeared to have had hot pies and baked potatoes.

"Hello, Hotspur," I said. "Hello, Jennifer." I found it difficult to speak to Anne.

"Where have you been?" It was Percy who spoke first, and he was reproachful.

"I've been working, Percy. Those planes don't fly themselves."

"Anne was ill."

"I know."

"It was only a broken arm and a few bruises," Anne said, mildly. I looked for the same reproach in her eyes but she was as impassive as ever. I would have preferred it if she had reproached me and called me out for my negligence.

"I just came to see how you are," I said. I wanted to sit

down with them – the ground was hard and dry – but I had not yet earned my place in their circle. "What brings you all out here on such a cold day?"

"Mother and I are leaving tomorrow," Anne explained. "So I came here to try to decide what to do with the house. Percy and Jennifer have been helping me make my decision."

"What have you decided?"

"I'd rather like to burn it down," she said, bitterness creeping into her voice.

"No!" Percy and Jennifer cried together.

Before I could respond, Henry came out of the shrubbery. He indicated to Percy and Jennifer that he was going back to the mainland and that they had to go with him.

"Aw…" They both intoned.

"I'm not ready to go back," said Percy, folding his arms.

"Well, I am," said Henry. "So you'd best come now or you'll have to carry your own wheelchair." I think that was the most I'd ever heard him say too. But I also realised from his voice how much he cared for my friend, Hotspur. He was always there for the boy, letting him have as much freedom as possible, whilst ensuring no harm ever came to him.

"You know I can't do that."

Amidst much complaining, Henry scooped Percy up, and took him and Jennifer to the boat. I realised that what he really intended was to give Anne and me some privacy.

I sat down next to her. The ground was much colder than I'd imagined. She laughed. "Maudie says we'll get piles."

"Do you really want to burn the house down?" I asked.

She nodded. "It's a vile place. It only makes the people who live in it unhappy."

"The Sullivans weren't unhappy when they stayed," I pointed out. "In fact, after Bunty's death, they were very happy."

"Perhaps it's only the Lakehams who have to suffer, then," Anne conceded. "For the sins of our ancestors. There are some real rogues and villains amongst them."

"I don't believe that, Anne. You're not responsible for what your relatives did in the past. None of us are. It's just a house, made of stone, like any other house."

"That's why I've decided to sell it. I'll give someone else the chance to be happy in it. Besides, Mother and I need the money if we're to live abroad."

"I thought…" I coughed, unsure whether to proceed.

"That I was an heiress?" She smiled, but it did not reach her eyes. "There is no money. Just the house, which leaks money. It's almost falling down and I can't afford to maintain it. The only money I have is what I've earned from my business. It's enough for now, but I will have to go back to work again in about a year."

"I wish I'd known that before," I said.

"Is that why you've stayed away? Because you thought I had money?" She frowned. "That doesn't make sense."

"Yes, it does, because I think my father was only following the money and I'm not him."

Anne shook her head. "Oh, no, Guy, you're very wrong. Your father knew there was no money. He looked into the whole estate. He still wanted to be with my mother. I only wish I'd been kinder to him, but perhaps it's in the Lakehams' nature to be possessive with those we love." She shivered.

"I'm sorry, Anne." I turned my head to face her. "I'm sorry I didn't support you more when you were in prison, and I'm sorry I've stayed away now."

"What else could you do when I had confessed to the murder of your father?"

"I could have believed the best of you instead of the worst."

"But you got onto Doctor Aitken somehow. Why did you realise he was behind it all?"

"Little things. His tendency to cast suspicion on others. The fact that there is nowhere for him to hide behind the curtain in the library, so he must have been listening from somewhere else."

"The secret door?"

"You might not have noticed it open if the room was dim. That gave me another idea. On the day I arrived, the doctor was already on the terrace waiting for us. He refused your offer to get his luggage, saying he would get it himself, yet I never once saw him with a suitcase. When Percy found the secret door it proved it to me."

"He was already in the house when we arrived," Anne said. She scoffed lightly. "He was living on the upper floors to be close to my mother. I never thought of that."

"On the day he supposedly arrived, he came via the secret door and waited on the terrace until someone found him there so he could pretend he had just turned up. Or perhaps he was going to walk around to the front door but we found him first. Either way, he was already here."

"She trusted him…" Anne mused. "That's one thing I don't understand."

"He kept her in medication, Anne, so she became reliant upon him."

"I never want to be that reliant on a man," she said.

That told me! "No, I don't suppose you do."

"I'd better get back." She stood up and brushed the dust off her skirt. Her hair gleamed in the winter sunshine. Gone was the platinum blonde and in its place was burnished copper. Freckles covered her small nose. This, I felt, was the real Anne, and I wished I had more time to get to know her, but it seemed she would not allow that.

We walked down to the boats. "Don't come up to the house, Guy," she said. "Give me time to get across the lake and then just leave. Please."

"Very well." It was no less than I deserved. Percy was right. I had failed to be the hero I should have been. "If that's what you want."

"I just can't bear another goodbye. I've already had to say it to Percy and Jennifer."

She climbed into a boat and took up the oars. "Thank you for coming," she said. "It helps. It really does."

"Will you ever forgive me?" I asked.

"I don't know yet…" She began to row. "I need more

time. I still have nightmares about Edith Thompson; only in the dream it's me…"

"Anne…" I closed my eyes. I'd had the same dream.

"No, don't. It's not your fault. None of it is. You lost your father before you even knew him."

"So did you."

"Yes… Yes, I suppose I did. Aitken stole both our fathers. So I want you to know that I don't blame you for anything." She began to row. She was only going across the lake and I could have followed her. I could have run after her on the opposite bank, taking her into my arms and begging her forgiveness. Perhaps that was what she hoped I would do. Was I failing again by not going after her?

She was halfway across the lake when she stopped and stood up.

"Guy!"

"Yes, Anne!"

"We're going to Venice first. We'll be there over Christmas."

"That will be nice for you," I said flatly.

"Oh Guy! I don't know if there's anywhere you can land your plane but… Can't you see I'm inviting you, you fool?"

"Oh." I ran my hands through my hair. "Damn. Wait there! I mean it, Anne. Wait for me or, so help me God, I'll chase you all across the world, let alone this bloody lake!" It seemed that not only the Lakehams could be possessive. I saw her throw her head back and laugh and knew that I had, at last, said the right thing.

I jumped into the other boat and rowed as if my life depended upon it. In fact it did. I knew that without this woman I would never be the man I wanted to be. Perhaps that was what my father felt when he met her mother. I wanted to believe that. It was the only way we could both move on and find our own way in life.

When I drew alongside her, I practically threw myself into her boat. She was crying and laughing at the same time. I fell into her waiting arms and at last knew that I was home.

Percy Sullivan

So that was it. My first crime and I solved it. I had help from Guy, I suppose. And Eleanor Grace, who pretty much told me everything when we found her chamber. But I revealed the killer. Everyone says so. I think I could get used to this. I just need to find another murder. They're a bit thin on the ground.

My English teacher was very impressed when I showed him my files, though he says that if I don't burn my thesaurus, he's going to get a doctor to surgically remove it.

I suppose I should say what happened to everyone after. Well, Mother and Father went off on a second honeymoon and now I'm going to have a new sister or brother. Jennifer's mother and father did the same. She's not having a new sister or brother, but she stayed with us whilst they were away.

It was lucky that when Anne and the doctor fell that he was underneath her and broke her fall. She did have a broken arm and some bruises, but she didn't die, which is the main thing.

Her mother looked much better when we visited. She came to say hello to us briefly, but soon went away again. Then we went to the island with Anne, even though it was cold.

"I spend a lot of time here, remembering that picnic," she told us as we shivered in our winter clothes. "I'm thinking of burning the house down," she said suddenly.

We argued about it, of course, but I don't really blame her after all the terrible things that have happened. I wanted to know what she was going to say to Guy when he turned up, but Henry dragged us away.

"I'm never going to fall in love," Jennifer said as Henry rowed us back to the main bank. "It seems like nothing but trouble."

Well, that was what she said then. But yesterday I had a letter from her saying that she had met a boy at her friend's house, called Peter, and that he was the dreamiest boy she had ever met. "It's real love, Percy. I know I can tell you this, as we are just friends. Aren't we?"

I'm so glad I didn't do anything stupid and tell her that, actually, I loved her.

Mother said not to worry. "There'll be other girls, darling."

"Plenty more fish in the sea," Father said.

"Not for boys like me," I told them.

"Of course there will," Mother insisted. "Lots of women are married to men in wheelchairs, especially since the war. But as you're only fourteen, I wouldn't worry about it too much now."

She's probably right. And perhaps Jennifer will come back when she's bored with Peter. I really liked solving crimes with her even if she did think she knew it all.

Oh, I forgot. I had a letter from Anne and Guy. They're married now and are going to move into Lakeham Abbey.

'Guy is going to turn part of the grounds into an airfield,' Anne said in her letter. *'And I'm going to set up a school for domestic help. We hope to turn the Abbey into a happy, productive place.'*

So everyone gets the girl but me...

We're going to Egypt this summer to join Father on a dig. I bet there'll be loads of murderous activity over there to keep me occupied (engaged, employed).

THE END

Fantastic Books
Great Authors

CROOKED
CAT

Meet our authors and discover our exciting range:

- Gripping Thrillers
- Cosy Mysteries
- Romantic Chick-Lit
- Fascinating Historicals
- Exciting Fantasy
- Young Adult and Children's Adventures

Printed in Great Britain
by Amazon